Praise for *The Lonely Ones*

"Spare and poignant, every word of this haunting and elegant novel in verse feels painstakingly selected....Fain's story is simply a brilliantly crafted coming-of-age novel that will appeal to the hearts and minds of all readers who have ever felt alone."

—*Kirkus Reviews* (starred review)

"The lyrical free verse style moves the narrative swiftly along. . . . Gorgeous writing distinguishes this short, but not shallow, read."

—*School Library Journal*

"This novel in free verse is exactly what a poetic novel should be . . . an immersive novel, like any good tale in which readers can take any individual poem and examine it in depth for word use, rhythm, and meaning."

—VOYA

Praise for *Where Silence Gathers*

"A poignant, heart-wrenching story of grief, love, and loss."
—*School Library Journal*

Praise for *Some Quiet Place*

"Sutton provides a creative and refreshingly original approach to the supernatural genre with well-developed characters and rich description... This intense roller-coaster ride of palpable emotions and suspense will keep readers engrossed from start to finish."

—*School Library Journal*

gardenia

KELSEY SUTTON

DIVERSIONBOOKS

Diversion Books
A Division of Diversion Publishing Corp.
443 Park Avenue South, Suite 1008
New York, New York 10016
www.DiversionBooks.com

This is a work of fiction. Names, characters, places and incidents either are the product of the author's imagination or are used fictitiously. Any resemblance to actual persons, living or dead, events or locales is entirely coincidental.

For more information, email info@diversionbooks.com

First Diversion Books edition February 2017.
Print ISBN: 978-1-62681-841-5
eBook ISBN: 978-1-68230-590-4

This one is for Gabs.

Chapter One

My eyes open. It takes a moment to realize that I'm not staring up at the ceiling of my room.

Instead, I'm standing beneath the last working street-light in the park, right in the center of its glow. I wrap my arms around myself as a shield from the cold, looking at her trailer with an empty feeling in my stomach. I must have walked in my sleep again. It seems to be getting worse over time, not better. Dimly I notice that I'm not wearing shoes. My toes curl under, scraping against the gravel. My boxer shorts snap in the wind. The air has teeth and nails. It's October and another Minnesota winter is coming. But I don't care.

The lights are off in her room, of course, along with all the others. She's been gone since July. I stare at her dark window, knowing I should go back to bed.

But I don't move. For minutes or hours—I'm not sure which—I just linger in the cold, another spirit haunting this place. It's something I've done dozens of times since we buried her. I've gotten used to the stiffness afterward, the absolute silence, the exhaustion.

Only when the sky turns purple and light reaches over the horizon with luminescent fingers do I turn to go back to my own trailer.

It's seventeen steps back. Fog hovers over the ground. Just as I reach the steps, an engine turns over in the distance—one of the neighbors must be going to work. The stillness is further disrupted by Madonna's voice blaring through the trailer as soon as I open our front door.

There's a stale smell in the air because no one has bothered to clean the parrot's cage this week. Spencer Hille perks up as I come in, his green feathers ruffled and gleaming. "I missed you!" he squawks.

I lumber down the narrow hall. The orange carpet is so thin I can feel the cool metal beneath it. Madonna continues to serenade the morning. "Mom." I knock on her door. It rattles on its hinges. "Your alarm is going off. Get up." I'm turning toward my room before the words have completely left my mouth.

She swears, and there's a slam as she assaults the snooze button. She'll keep doing it if I don't wake her up myself. Sighing, I turn back around. The carpet does nothing to muffle the moans of the floor as I approach the door again. "Five more minutes!" Mom thunders.

I push my way into her room. There's a pile of Dad's junk behind the door—an antique clock that doesn't work anymore, some Stephen King books, clothes, a pair of mounted antlers. I pat around looking for the light, which has become nearly impossible to find since Mom nailed a blanket over her window. I feel the switch and flip it up without hesitation.

My mother utters a sound that a vampire might make in direct sunlight. She yanks the sheets higher. "You have to be at the diner in a half hour," I tell her pitilessly. A middle finger pokes out. The alarm goes off again. Mom emerges from the covers, opening bloodshot eyes.

The numbers over her head glow brightly, and, as always, the seconds continue to count down. Annie Erickson will be alive for another thirty years, seven months, nine days, two hours, thirty-eight minutes, and twenty-seven seconds.

That's how I know waking up at 7:30 a.m. won't kill her.

Groaning, Mom manages to find the snooze button a second time. Once it's silenced she buries her face in the pillow. The latest Danielle Steel novel rests on her nightstand. "Is this one any good?" I ask, picking it up and glancing at the back cover.

"Give me five more minutes," she mumbles.

"I'm going to the nursing home before school. You need to get up now."

She calls me a name, hot and foul. "That's sweet," I tell her. "Get up." For good measure, I turn the stereo on before leaving. I head for the bathroom and pass my sister's door, which is tightly shut. There's no reason to wake her; running a website requires no set hours. I wash my face and water dampens the front of my shirt. After patting dry with a towel, I brush my teeth and re-enter the hall with the taste of mint in my mouth.

In front of the cracked mirror hanging over my dresser—Vanessa broke it when we were nine, spinning so fast to a Britney Spears song that she knocked it off the wall—I braid my hair as well as I possibly can. Frizzy curls always manage to escape. I don't bother with makeup before putting my glasses on; my skin is clear, the one and only noticeable quality I have. Numbers above me glow like all the others, but the mirror is strategically angled so I can't see anything above my forehead.

Next I move to the closet and root around for some jeans. As I yank on a turtleneck and some boots, I notice a huge hole in the knee. No time to change, though, and these are probably the last clean pair anyway. I grab my bag, listening for the familiar jangle of keys, and go.

"You're beautiful!" Spencer Hille calls as I rush by.

My '96 Buick is waiting outside. It may not be a pretty vehicle, but it's faithful, turning over on the first try. The smell of gas permeates the air. I wait for the frost on the windshield to melt a bit before driving out of the trailer park. Just as the tires bump onto the main road, I notice the rearview mirror has been tilted. Lorna must have gone out after I went to bed last night. I quickly readjust it so the reflection only shows my eyes and the sign for the park, GREEN ESTATES. Except when George Blue was sixteen he painted over the E so now it reads WELCOME TO GREEN PROSTATES.

George is now our mayor.

The sign fades behind me, and soon enough Hallett Cottages appears on my right. It's the only place in Kennedy for the elderly, combining a nursing home and an assisted living facility. I started volunteering when I was nine, reading to the residents or helping them with meals. The building is nondescript, with brown brick and ancient square windows. The trees have been cleared around it, making the poorly-tended lawn its most noticeable quality. I guide my car into the usual space, park, cut the engine, and step out into the cold again. The leaves on the trees are vibrant hues of orange and red and yellow. They rustle a greeting to me as I walk inside.

Rita, the front desk nurse, nods as the doors slide open. In all the time I've known her, she has never smiled. "Getting chilly," she says by way of greeting.

I shrug ruefully, writing my name on the check-in list. "We knew it was coming, right?"

Steam rises from the cup of coffee by her hand. My stomach rumbles as I head straight for the third room on the left to visit a woman who is always up at the crack of dawn.

Miranda Raspberry is seventy-three years old. She's one of the youngest residents of Hallett. She's also one of my favorites. I knock on the door and a soft voice warbles, "Come in." I enter the bright space. Miranda sits on her perfectly made bed. "Oh, Hannah," the tiny woman exclaims, beaming. She sets her knitting down. Her gray hair curls against her head, and she's wearing pink pants with a sweatshirt. Gene Simmons peers at me from the worn material. "I was just thinking about you."

"Hi, Mom." Smiling, I take her proffered hand and note that she's attempted to paint her nails. Pink polish stains the skin around them. The walls are covered with needlepoint creations and the air smells like perfume. I look around for the hundredth time, savoring it as I always do because this will all be gone soon, as if no one named Miranda Raspberry ever lived here.

After a few moments I realize that Miranda is frowning at me. "Honey, what in the world are you wearing?" She pinches my clothes between two fingers. The pink chair by her window is a familiar place, and I like to think that the cushion recognizes me as an old friend. I sink down and it lets out a *whoosh* of air.

I don't answer for a moment; I'm distracted by the numbers above her. In stark, white, unavoidable truth, they tick down. Miranda Raspberry has twenty-eight days, nineteen hours, seventeen minutes, and fifty-six seconds to live. "I'm auditioning for a play today. This is a costume."

Her expression clears and she's back to smiling. "You are? You never told me you had an interest in acting!"

Acting, pretending, it's all the same. I open my mouth to describe the supposed play, but before I can, Miranda stiffens. There's a sudden shadow in her eyes, and lines deepen around her mouth. "You're not Hannah." She stands. Her voice has lost its warmth, and now she sounds like a small, lost child. The tile creaks.

I remain calm. "No, Mrs. Raspberry. I'm not. I'm Ivy."

She glances at the door behind her, as if she's thinking about fleeing. "Where's Hannah?" she whispers. "Where am I?"

This isn't the first time she's been lucid. It happens at least once a week. But she never remembers that her daughter and her husband died in a car accident back in 1983. Some people might tell her the truth: she's utterly alone. But I see the time she has left. This is why I come to Hallett—to create happy endings. So once again I sit back to tell Miranda Raspberry of a beautiful, fictitious past she can't remember.

It's better than talking about the future I know she won't have.

Chapter Two

Everyone has moved on.

I make my way through the halls of Kennedy High, holding my books close and trying to tune out all the chatter around me. While I am still stuck in a day that happened over two months ago, while I keep thinking that Vanessa will never experience her senior year of high school, the only thing my peers want to talk about is the new girl. Apparently she moved here from Minneapolis and she was kicked out of her old school. There was once a time when I would have been just as curious. Now no one will look me in the eye, much less tell me the latest town gossip.

Well, not *no one*. My gaze meets Brent Nordstrom's—the sheriff's stepson—for an instant before skittering away. Most people I would glare at or make some snarky comment to, but not him. I can feel his stare boring into my back as I hurry to class. Just seeing Brent makes me feel nauseous.

The door swings shut behind me, a welcome barrier. Like every other day, I go through the motions. Taking notes in astronomy. Listening to the teacher talk about a script during drama. A discussion about *Of Mice and Men* throughout English. I write so hard in my notebook that the words sink into the page beneath. The empty desk in each room still doesn't escape my notice.

I see her everywhere. I hear her voice. *So serious, Ivy. Come on, live a little.* All the while those numbers over her head ticked down, down, down, and there was nothing I could do.

"…had many obstacles to overcome. Does anyone have an idea what those obstacles were? Ivy?" Ms. Jones asks.

I try to shove Vanessa out of my head.

During lunch I sit in a corner, picking at the lasagna. A group of children sit farther down the table; our community is so small that all grades share the building. The clock on the wall taunts me and I lower my gaze. I'm so absorbed in the contours of the tray that I don't see the shadow standing over me until it's too late. A moment later milk splatters over all my food, onto the table, and soaks into my pants. I jump up and look at Mitch Donovan. He has the same bright eyes, the same red hair as his twin sister. It's still like seeing a ghost every time.

"I would tell you to go fuck yourself, but I'm pretty sure you'd be disappointed," I say through my teeth.

He doesn't say anything. He doesn't smile, smirk, or insult me. He just clutches the milk carton in his hand— the cardboard crumples loudly—then turns his back and walks to his table.

Everyone is staring now, which I absolutely loathe. I hurry to dump my tray and flee the cafeteria.

After school I drive to Nick's, where I work part-time as

a dishwasher. It's the only place in town that will hire me…
and that's only because my uncle happens to own the place.

The bell over the door jingles as I push it open. A gust
of air hits me, laden with the scent of grease and coffee. The
dinner rush hasn't started yet and most of the booths are
empty. The chrome counters are clean and stocked.

Mom is standing at the far side of the room, nodding at something Hubert Gill is saying. His hands move
emphatically as he speaks. He owns the local grocery store
and has a longtime crush on my mother. At the sound of
the bell Mom gives me a distracted wave. She looks tired
and a bit exasperated. Wisps of hair fall into her eyes and
her mint-green uniform is wrinkled. Susie—Nick's other
waitress and my godmother—cheerfully smacks an order
on the counter. I wave back to Mom and head straight for
the office to clock in.

"Ivy!" Amar shouts from the kitchen, raising his spatula
in a salute. A burger hisses on the grill. His eyes gleam with
excitement. "Did you know your heart beats one hundred
thousand times in one day?"

"Keep the fun facts coming, Amar." I wink and walk
past the kitchen doorway, into the narrow back hall.

The office door is open, so I go in. Smoke hovers in
the air and tickles my throat. Uncle Nick looks up from his
paperwork. "Hey, kid," he says around the cigarette in his
mouth. "How was school?"

"Typical." I jam my card in and out of the stamper
before putting it back. I reach for a clean apron on the
wall hook and drop it over my head, reaching back to tie
the strings. Thankfully, it covers the milk splotch on my

jeans. "You know you're not supposed to smoke in here," I chide halfheartedly.

He inhales. "Hank wouldn't fail me. I've known him since he was three."

Hank is the current health inspector. Since he, too, smokes like a chimney, I don't think this place is in much danger of being shut down. I change the subject. "Do you mind if I leave a little early today? I want to go to the nursing home before visiting hours are over."

My uncle raises his brows at me. There's a trail of ashes across his desk. "Again? How many times does that make this week?"

"What can I say? They're the only people that can stand me." I shrug, as if it doesn't matter.

Nothing fools Uncle Nick. He gives me a knowing look, tightening his grip on a pen with one beefy fist. He takes one more long drag of his cigarette and then crushes the glowing orange tip on the ashtray with his other hand. "This town is full of idiots, kid. You won't be here forever. Remember that. Hey, how about we go on another fishing trip soon?"

They're kind words, meant to encourage, but they have the opposite effect. Because the fact is, I'm never going to leave Kennedy. I'll never escape this place. I'm destined to be trapped among this hate and death and pain for the rest of my life.

While I struggle to give him an optimistic response, my uncle bends to open a drawer. The numbers hovering over him move into my line of sight before I can look away. Nick Erickson has one month, twenty-seven days, four hours, fifty-nine minutes, and two seconds to live. Those numbers are the reason why I've never hesitated to love or grow close to this man.

He doesn't know it, but Uncle Nick and I are going to die on the same day.

Chapter Three

The numbers have been there my entire life.

I've always wondered why I'm the only one to be tormented by their glowing knowledge. I've hated them and fought a futile fight against them. There were times I delved into my past, even the details of my birth, to find out why I see what no one else sees. In secret I have gone to psychics and called neurosurgeons. Most of them were dead ends; I wasted precious money for empty babbling about gifts or mental disorders. One doctor had an interesting theory about neural processes, but I quickly hung up when he asked for my name.

The only real answer I could come up with is that some of us are just born cursed.

I didn't know what the numbers were, though, until my grandmother had a heart attack in front of me. I was three, and had learned to count down from ten. I still remember sitting on the orange carpet with my Barbie dolls. The TV was on. Grandma was standing at the counter in the kitchen. The phone was lodged between her ear and shoulder as she chopped some cucumbers. "Grandma, watch me count your numbers!" I called. "Nine, eight, seven," I said to my Barbies. "Six, five, four, three, two, one!"

Grandma dropped the phone. It clattered to the floor.

"Ivy," she gasped, clutching her chest. She grabbed at the counter with her other hand, but she missed and fell down beside the phone. Thinking it was a game, I laughed and hurried across those diamond-shaped tiles to reach her.

"Grandma, you're zero," I told her, shaking her shoulder. I leaned close and the smell of her flowery perfume teased my nostrils. "Grandma?"

She didn't answer.

• • •

In the distance, a familiar whistle shrieks.

I fumble for my glasses on the nightstand. The red numbers on the alarm clock come into focus. Whenever it passes our town, the train arrives at exactly 2:29. It's an ugly thing that rushes through the darkness, shamed by all the vulgar scribbles and drawings running along the side of the cars.

I rake my hair back and force myself to rise from bed. Forgetting about a stack of books on the floor, I stub my toe and muffle a curse. The music of my mother's snores doesn't falter and the fan in my sister's room hums. It's enough for me, so I pull my boots on.

Clad in sweatpants and a T-shirt, I open the window and swing one leg over the sill. Gravel crunches underfoot.

The rest of the world sleeps on; I can see lights from town in the distance, few and faint. The windows of the nine other trailers are dark.

White plumes swirl from my mouth with every breath, but there's no time to go back for the coat I've forgotten yet again. That single light in the park flickers and watches as I hunch over and weave through the shadows. The sound of barking shatters the stillness. Mrs. Jones's dog claws at her door, wanting out. "Quiet, Idiot!" I hiss, rushing past. He whines.

Soon the grass of the field tickles my knees. The train depot is just under a mile away. I've visited so many times that a slight trail has formed. Blinking the last dregs of sleep from my eyes, I follow the familiar dirt path grooved into the weeds. The trees rustle and murmur my name. It's comforting, as though they've been waiting.

More lights appear ahead. My pace quickens in anticipation. Most people find the depot frightening; it's been abandoned for years. I don't know why the train stops here when there are no shipments, no loads or goods or passengers for the cars to unload. Maybe there were, years ago, and no one bothered to change its pattern. I've accepted it as yet another mystery in the strange story that is my life. The solitude, the quiet purpose, is something I look forward to every time the train comes.

I rush toward where my paint is hidden—beneath the counter in the drafty office. But then I stop. The depot is not empty tonight. Through the grimy window, I see something that does not belong.

There's a body on the tracks.

I abandon the paint and run back out the door. My

feet pound against the frozen ground. I get close enough to make out more details, and moonlight reveals that it's a girl lying there. She's alive; the numbers tick above her head. "What are you doing?" I call out, relieved and irritated.

The girl doesn't shout, doesn't twitch, doesn't even open her eyes at the abrupt sound of my voice. She just continues to rest on the metal rods and planks of wood as if it is the most natural, comfortable place to be. Her chest rises and falls slowly. She isn't afraid. Doesn't she realize that the train will move again, as it always does? I approach her, still frowning, and look down at her face. She must know I'm here, but she ignores me. The timer suspended over her has eighty-two years, one month, one day, six hours, twenty-four minutes, and eleven seconds left.

For a moment I study her dark, greasy dreadlocks and the bridge of freckles over her nose. A silver stud peeks out from one of her nostrils. This is the new girl that everyone's been talking about. We have two classes together.

"You're from Minneapolis, right? What's your name again?" I ask. The words echo through the depot. The wind's ferocity increases, as if it wants to know as well.

Finally the girl speaks, but she doesn't even open her eyes. "Amanda Ryan. Who are you?"

"Ivy Erickson," I answer, glowering now. Dew clings to my skin. "This is my spot. Go find your own."

Her hands are folded over her stomach and her legs are crossed at the ankles. Her tone is as languid as her posture as she replies, "There wasn't a sign saying this was private property."

"It isn't," I snap.

Now she opens her eyes. They're a bright green that I

instantly envy when I compare them to the pale, watery blue of my own. "Then how is it your spot?" she counters.

She has me there. Wistfully I think of my paint, of everything I could do tonight on the metal canvas of the train cars. Right now there is nothing on the one I have my eye on, just the word BITCH scrawled over the surface in violent purple. But I can't paint with someone watching. I sigh and sit down beside the new girl. "Why'd you come to Kennedy?" I ask next, less hostile.

Amanda closes her eyes again. "My caseworker thought it would be a healthy change from the city."

She's dressed more intelligently than I am. A thick coat protects her from the cold, and jeans hug her slim hips. The tips of her Converse shoes glow in the near-blackness. The laces are undone. I don't tell her, though; somehow I don't think she cares. "Do you make it a habit to drape yourself across active train tracks?"

A crease appears between her brows. Annoyance. "Chatty, aren't you, Ivy Erickson?"

I shrug. "Not usually. Just when I find people in my depot in the middle of the night. You're thinking about killing yourself, aren't you?"

This startles her. Maybe it's the directness of it, or maybe because she's never heard the truth uttered out loud. I watch her take me in. My awkward body, my sharp features, my frizzy hair, the fogged glasses perched on my nose. "I've heard about you," she says. "The other kids said you're insane. That you used to do more than lay on some train tracks."

I open my mouth to respond. Suddenly the train lets out a loud hiss. Amanda jumps, as if she wasn't really expecting it to happen. She turns her attention to the ugly beast now. Unceremoniously, I get up and brush my butt off. I turn away from the new girl. "Don't come back here," I toss over my shoulder as I walk away. "Like I said, this is my spot." The stars chide me for being rude, but I ignore them.

Her voice follows me. "Don't you care that I might be about to die?"

"You won't," I say simply.

Life is so wasted on the living.

Chapter Four

I watch him from behind a tree. Where I watch him every Saturday morning.

He crosses the lumberyard to talk to his boss. He listens and nods, frowning. He didn't brush his hair this morning—I can tell. His brown curls are wild, falling into his eyes. At least he made the effort to grab a coat. It's the one I gave him last Christmas, the green parka. I dig my fingers into the bark, missing him so much it hurts.

Myers Patripski. My ex-boyfriend.

As always, I can feel time working against me. I want so badly to be unaware of the seconds passing, but for me, it's impossible. He'll be leaving soon. Getting into his truck and going home. I hate standing here, staring like someone desperate and insane. When it comes to Myers, I lose all my nerve. This is the only way I can see him since he graduated last year and rarely ventures into town. He would never miss work, though. Myers may be many things, but negligent isn't one of them.

It's as if he can feel my longing, because he looks toward the woods. I shrink back. At that moment, the clouds break and sunlight hits the ground. Myers squints. It's easy to envision the rich chocolate hue of his irises. I stand in the shadows and think of his lips, his hands, the way they felt on my skin.

I turn away before Myers does. A branch snaps beneath my boot as I begin the walk back to my car. A bird whistles at me overhead, one of the few left in this part of the world. Leaves are withering and falling faster now. Their delicate veins are sad smiles.

Vanessa died in the woods.

Though it was miles from here, in another forest entirely, the thought won't leave me alone now. I start to run.

When I get back, Mom's car isn't parked next to the trailer. She must be pulling a double at the diner. Idiot barks as I climb the stairs and shoulder the front door open. It sticks sometimes.

My sister is awake.

"Hey," she mumbles around a mouthful of cereal. She's sitting at the table—there's just a small spot clear of junk so only one of us can use it at a time—and she's unabashedly wearing the lingerie she must have displayed on her site last night.

"Can't you put some clothes on?" I brush past her to open the fridge.

Lorna doesn't bother answering, but Spencer Hille yelps, "You're gorgeous!" He picks at the bars of the cage with his beak.

"We really should teach the damn parrot some other words." I take a package of string cheese out of the drawer.

As I chew, Lorna croons at him and drops a Cheerio at his feet. "It's sweet," she argues. I put the cheese back. "My self-esteem has definitely improved since we found him."

I lean against the wall and watch her for a moment. Lorna and Mom got all the beauty in the family. The long legs, the tame hair, the striking features. Just like the rest of Kennedy, Lorna could have been so much more. It would be one thing if the website made her happy, but even a stranger could see that it doesn't. She has one fatal flaw: laziness. School was too much work. So was leaving. Still, my sister has fifty-seven years, two months, one day, forty-five minutes, and thirty-three seconds to waste. I feel my eyes narrow with resentment. Lorna doesn't even notice. She's reading an old copy of *People* magazine. As I continue to stare, she turns the page. The only thing I'd personally find interesting in that magazine was whether or not Brad Pitt would live to make another movie. Unfortunately, when it comes to TV and print, I can't see the numbers. Stupid curse.

"See you later," I mutter, creaking down the hallway to my room. If Lorna replies, I don't hear it. Once inside, I make sure to close and lock the door. I get down on my knees and reach under the bed, feeling for the familiar ridge of a box. It slides out easily. For a few seconds I just look down at the cardboard tabs, then I take a breath and force myself to pull them apart.

It's everything I've been able to compile in the last two and a half months. No easy task. For some of it I had to bribe Fred, a new deputy who graduated the same year as Myers. It wasn't cheap. Eyewitness reports, phone records, and evidence lists, on top of newspaper articles I clipped and websites I scoured.

It's still hard to look at the pictures. Her eyes are wide and unblinking. Glassy. There's blood in her hair and bruises on her throat. Her fingers are curled and one leg is bent beneath her. She rests on a bed of green-brown leaves, and she's wearing her pajamas: a lace tank and matching shorts. The pink flowers are stark against the paleness of her skin. I swallow, spreading the images out until they're all on the carpet in front of me.

There has to be something the sheriff's people missed.

My eyes skim each page for the hundredth time. *Found in Havenger's Woods. 1 a.m. Time of death estimated at 11 p.m. Crushed windpipe, head wound. Tip made by Ivy Erickson.* I lean over, tangling my hands in my hair. There *has* to be something I'm missing. Each picture is bright, illuminated by a camera's flash.

"Ivy? Are you all right?"

There's a knock on my door. Lorna. Concerned. Why? That's when I realize I'm crying. "I'm fine," I say dully, staring down at the pictures. Lorna isn't the kind to linger. The floor groans at her retreat, then the sound of my sister enclosing herself in that room once again. She can lose herself so easily in seduction and computer screens. All I have, all I'm consumed by, is this. My attention never wavers from the nightmare at my knees. I swipe at my wet nose and rake my hair back, mindless of the mess I'm leaving in the strands. "You're beautiful!" Spencer Hille cries for the millionth time. The words echo down the hall. I barely hear him.

I need to know what happened. I need to find the murderer. I need to find out the truth. Not just for Vanessa. Not just for her family. For me.

Because everyone in Kennedy thinks I know who killed her.

Chapter Five

Now I notice Amanda Ryan in class.

During astronomy she sits at the very back of the room, hood drawn up over her tangled hair, and doesn't bother to hide the fact that she's falling asleep. I can't help but glance at her throughout the lecture, wondering why she wants to die. Not when so many others wish to live. The numbers over that hood tell me that she won't kill herself, though. No, Amanda Ryan will die when she's ninety-nine.

But Shannon Wyoming won't last that long. She sits in front of me every day, blissfully unaware of her impending fate, just like the rest of them. When the leaves are turning green again and the warm breezes return, the beautiful cheerleader will join me, Vanessa, Uncle Nick, my grandmother, Miranda Raspberry, and everyone else with small numbers. She'll only be eighteen years old. Too young, just like the rest of us. There's no hope of saving her.

I silence the faint voice in my head that hopes she goes on the day of the sale she's currently babbling about.

"Ivy Erickson. Can you tell me what I just said?"

I twist around and meet Mrs. Parker's eyes. I know we've been talking about stars. Dying stars. Some go quietly, some end their lives in an explosion of brilliance. What Mrs. Parker doesn't know is that there's no point in me learning it. "Stars," I answer lamely. She comes to stand beside my desk, and looks down at me with a disapproving purse of her lips. I focus on the cross she's wearing around her neck. It glints in the light.

"Did you read the chapters I assigned on Friday?"

This time I don't attempt a response. Because, really, we both know the answer. Someone snickers. I glance toward the sound, a reflex. Brent and Mitch sit side by side. The heat of their gazes burns me. My hands form fists under the desk. Mrs. Parker says something else that I don't hear, but I do notice one of the other girls giggling. "Where's your off button?" I snap at her. The sound cuts short in her throat and her eyes widen.

Mrs. Parker sighs. "Go to the office, Ivy. There's no point of you being in my class if you aren't really here."

She's right. There's no point.

No point at all.

• • •

I met Vanessa in kindergarten.

Back then I was quiet, shy, mousy. She was vibrant, brave, guileless. She wore a red dress with shining black shoes. I remember sitting at a tiny table, learning the months in the year as we recited them in unison. Vanessa was the loudest. Afterward, she came up to me. I was drawing with crayons. "You can go outside the lines," she said.

For a minute, she watched the movements of my hand. Eventually all I said was, "Show me."

That was the beginning.

We grew up. I spray-painted rusting train cars in the middle of the night, and Vanessa was crowned homecoming queen. I fell in love with Myers Patripski, the boy from the lumberyard, and Vanessa dated Brent Nordstrom, team quarterback. She surrounded herself with glittering friends and she was my only one. Her parents managed to pay all their bills and I worked in my uncle's diner to help Mom with hers. The Donovans went to Florida once a year and my family had yet to leave Kennedy. In almost every regard, Vanessa and I made no sense. But it worked.

Because every night we returned to the same place: our trailer park. She allowed me glimpses of the Vanessa Donovan no one else had. The insulin shots she had to take for her diabetes. The way she frowned at her body in the mirror. All her struggles with grades. How much she worried about what people thought of her. She saw glimpses of my darkest secrets, too. She knew about the pictures of my father that I kept under my mattress, safe from Mom's destruction, along with the locket he gave me when I was four. She knew about the resentment toward my mother and my sister. And she knew that there was something different about me, something that stopped me from getting close to others. Later, when I began to unravel and take risks with my life to taunt the numbers, she was right there beside me.

So all the differences were nothing. And, really, we

were most alike in the one way that mattered; we both had small numbers over our heads.

My best friend just didn't know it.

Chapter Six

Amar is hiding something.

He drops a pan into the sink, and his dimples are missing, his gaze averted. I set my dishrag down and frown at him. The pile beside me is higher than usual—detention put me behind—but I can't let this pass. "What's wrong?"

"Nothing!" he chirps, shoving at his sleeves even though they're already above his elbows. He's a terrible liar. Before I can interrogate him, the cook turns and heads back to his spot in front of the deep fryer. I release the plate in my hand and follow.

"Amar."

He says something under his breath in Arabic. "That boy is here," he mumbles reluctantly. It takes me a moment to realize who he means. My mouth goes dry. Myers. Of course.

It's strange to see Amar scowl, but no one at Nick's is a fan of Myers. Not since he dumped me almost three months ago. I make an effort to smile at him. "Don't worry,

Amar. I'm fine. I'm over him. You don't need to get so upset, okay?" He just keeps muttering unintelligible insults. I turn to go back to the sink, saying over my shoulder, "And *don't* spit in his food."

Mom comes huffing in. She takes one look at me and fixes her glare on Amar. He cowers. "You spilled the beans, didn't you?" she accuses him.

Suddenly Amar is consumed by flipping his burgers. "I bought a new book," he mumbles. "Did you know that hummingbirds flap their wings between fifty and seventy times a second?"

Mom sets some dishes down next to me with a clatter. "Are you all right, honey? I thought we made it pretty obvious last time we didn't want him around here. Stupid kid." She rubs my shoulder.

Again I manage to paste a smile across my face. "I'm fine," I repeat. The words lost meaning long ago. Mom gives me a look that says she doesn't buy it for a second. She calls Myers a name she usually reserves for me at 7:30 a.m.

"Annie!" Amar makes a sharp gesture to the plates of food he's set out for her. Mom glares as she takes them and hurries back out. Amar reaches for the knob on the radio to turn the volume up. As soon as his back is turned I slip away, out the door, and into the hall.

The diner is busy tonight. Uncle Nick has even left his office to stand beside a booth and talk to the sheriff. It feels like a layer of frost spreads over my skin when I see Allen McCork. He's in his uniform, his badge glinting weakly in the light. My mind barely registers that Brent is sitting beside him.

Allen was the one who began the flood of distrust

toward me. He brought me in for questioning because, the night Vanessa died, I spoke to her on the phone for eight seconds. I also happened to find her body, and when the police arrived, I was babbling hysterically about ominous notes in her room that were never found. To Allen, it all just seemed too convenient. There's also the fact that, over the years, Vanessa and I took more than one ride to the station in the back of his car. So even though I couldn't have been the one that killed her—the patterns of bruising on Vanessa's neck indicated someone with large hands, probably a male—people think I'm hiding who did. There wasn't enough evidence to build a case, and Mom drove us deeper into debt hiring a good lawyer. But the damage was still done.

Uncle Nick doesn't look pleased that the sheriff is here now, but I know he wouldn't go so far as to refuse service to Allen McCork. My uncle is not a man of confrontation. The only outward sign that he's agitated is the way his fingers twitch. Doubtless he'll be having a cigarette after this.

I seek out another face, one that also causes me turmoil, but of another kind entirely. I can't stop myself. Not when I know he's so near.

As soon as I see him, my heart skips a beat. It always does. He's sitting in a corner booth with some of his friends from the yard. No, not all of them are friends from the yard. There's a girl in the mix. I recognize her; she graduated last year, too. Ginger Marks. She's beautiful, like Lorna, with her confident demeanor and dainty features. She laughs at something Myers says, and it's unfair that someone should have such perfect teeth. I grip the corner of the wall, drowning in a wave of jealousy. Helpless, hopeless, my mind goes back to that night. The one that ended with my best friend dead in the woods and began with a betrayal.

Suddenly, just like that, I can't remember any of it—Myers is looking right at me. As if I'm standing behind my tree, watching the lumberyard, my fingers seek to dig into the bark. They meet wall instead, and pain radiates through my hand.

I can't breathe. I don't want to. Because just the slightest breath will break this spell. I think of those messages I left, those times I tried to get him to talk, those attempts at explanations and apologies, all rebuffed. I gave up quickly; I saw the futility of seeking forgiveness when there was no way of us ending well. It's better that he stays away. But if Myers hates me so much, why is he staring at me as if he wishes things were different, too?

Something crashes in the diner. I jump, glancing away from Myers. A woman—no, a girl, probably just a little older than me—quickly squats to pick up the pieces of a broken coffee cup. Her cheeks are flaming, and she's obviously an out-of-towner passing through, stopping for some caffeine. At first I give her only a cursory glance; I want to keep looking at Myers. But then my eyes fly back to her to take in the glowing numbers over the stocking cap she's wearing. The girl doesn't look up from the mess on the floor. My heart stutters and I stop breathing for the second time that night…but not because the boy I love sees me. I stare, not wanting to believe, but *the numbers don't lie.*

She's going to die in twenty-two minutes.

• • •

There's nothing I can do.

I know that. I know that.

But suddenly it doesn't matter.

The girl stammers an apology to my mom for the broken mug, who waves it off and pours her another coffee, in a to-go cup this time. Steam rises from the surface. The girl smiles gratefully at Mom as she puts the lid on, and she's so oblivious. She's wearing pink gloves—I don't know why that detail stands out the most to me. I continue to watch with rapt attention. How is she going to die? Will she slip on some ice? Will she step into the street?

There's a flash of an image in my mind: Vanessa's limp hand in the leaves. I swallow. So much death, so much knowledge, and I'm powerless.

Twenty-one minutes. Her time is running out. It can't be helped or stopped.

I still follow her.

The bell sings and a gust of wind hits me in the face. "Ivy?" I hear Mom call. "Where are you going?"

It's already dark out. The parking lot is empty, save for a few cars, and the girl is heading for a PT Cruiser in the far, shadowed corner. Out of sight from the diner windows. Her boot heels click on the pavement. Twenty minutes left now. I stand on the sidewalk, shivering, since I've foregone wearing a coat again. The headlights of the Cruiser flash and there's a click as she unlocks the doors.

I clench my fists. I'm going to watch her drive away. What else can I do?

Vanessa! Vanessa, answer me!

No. I won't let it happen again.

But before I can stop the girl from leaving, she turns

the key in the ignition and the starter whines. I run, expecting the engine to roar to life. It doesn't. The girl frowns and tries again. Another, longer whine. I reach her side and tap on the window with my knuckle. The girl shrieks. I wince, stepping back. Her expression changes from fright to relief, and her mouth moves as she says something. I shake my head, pointing at the glass between us. Quickly she hits the button and rolls it down. "Sorry," she says with a shaky laugh. "I probably had too much coffee today."

"There's a mechanic inside, if you're having car trouble," I tell her. "Want me to go get him?"

The girl rakes her bangs back with frustrated fingers. My attention is drawn once again to those pink gloves. "I only have ten bucks on me. This is great. Exactly what I needed."

"I don't think Ray would charge you," I reassure her, trying not to look at those numbers. Nineteen minutes. "Just…stay here, all right? Don't move. I'll get him." I spin back toward the diner.

"Thank you so much," she shouts after me. I give her a distracted wave in acknowledgment as I reach for the door handle and go back inside.

Leaving her all alone.

Chapter Seven

Myers isn't sitting in the booth anymore. I can't stop myself from noticing his empty spot as I hurry toward Ray Carson, the scruffy town drunk. The only reason his shop has remained open so long is because it happens to be the only one in Kennedy. The man sits alone, gazing down at his pancakes as if the meaning of life floats in the syrup.

I stop beside him, and he takes a few moments to focus on my face. His baseball cap does nothing to hide his red-rimmed eyes or sunken cheeks. "You're Annie's kid, right?" he says, slurring. Looks like old Ray has already had a few drinks tonight, then. Damn it.

"There's a girl out in the parking lot who needs you to take a look at her car," I tell him without preamble. Eighteen minutes.

He rubs the top of his bald head. "Needs my help, eh? You know who else needed my help? This damn country. Gave it sixteen years of my life, and what do I get? A bullet in my hip and a goddamn discharge. They couldn't even give me—"

This is a tirade I've heard many, many times before. "If you take a look at the car, I'll get you a piece of pie, all right, Ray?"

"Pie," he grumbles, hauling himself up. The table shudders. "I live for pie now."

"At least you'll live," I say without thinking. For another eleven years, seventeen days, six hours, twenty minutes, and thirty-seven seconds, at least.

He squints at me. "Huh?"

"Nothing. Here, let me help you."

"I don't want your help!" The old mechanic shakes me off. He mutters under his breath and brushes by. I follow him at a discreet distance.

Mom gives me a questioning look as I pass her. "Customer with car trouble," I offer by way of explanation. I don't give her a chance to respond. Seventeen minutes. Ray shoulders the door open and I inhale the fresh air with hope this time. It's snowing now. Lightly. It must have just started. Doubtless the transient snowflakes will swiftly give way to rain, as they often do during this time of year.

"Which way?" Ray snaps at me. I point to the rear parking lot. My heart pounds harder again. I need to find a way to stay by the girl, delay her leaving for the minutes remaining. I can call an ambulance, if need be. If she's just standing beside me, not driving or moving, nothing can reach her. Even death. Can it?

We circle the diner. Away from the windows and back into the darkness. I crane my neck to see her. "Which one is it, now?" Ray asks.

I barely hear him.

I've stopped in my tracks. My heart sinks into my stomach, and once again I don't want to accept what my eyes see. *No, no, no…* "Ivy?" Ray asks from a long distance. He sounds even more irritated.

The PT Cruiser is right where I left it.

And the girl is gone.

• • •

"I've never been so embarrassed in my life."

Idiot continues to bark even when the front door slams behind Mom and me. She tosses her purse onto the couch, then yanks off her coat and throws that down too.

"What about the time I was suspected of being an accomplice to murder? Or all the other times you had to bail me out?" I snap, turning the lock. It's quiet; Lorna must be doing her show.

"I missed you!" Spencer Hille chirps. He flaps his wings, and they make a *rat-a-tat* sound against the cage.

Mom pinches the bridge of her nose. She turns to face me. "Ivy…" That's it. Just my name. The syllables hold a thousand memories, shadows, pains, and I'm suddenly flooded by a wave of guilt. The same guilt that finally put a stop to the recklessness, the risks, the idiotic battle against my numbers. Whenever I'm tempted to do something— walk along the edge of a roof, stand too close to a fire, play chicken with an oncoming car—I hear her voice in my head the last time she picked me up from the station. *Why, Ivy?*

My mother has already had a hard life. It's evident in the lines under her eyes, the slump to her shoulders. Despite her flaws, she's done her best to take care of us. After Dad walked out, she stayed. She works day and night. She loses time and sleep and the pursuit of dreams.

Over her shoulder, I can see the bright reflection of my numbers in the living room window. In one month, twenty-four days, two hours, nineteen minutes, and five seconds, Annie Erickson will suffer two more losses. A brother. A daughter.

When I don't respond, Mom gives up on talking sense and goes to the answering machine. She tugs at the clip in her hair. I stand there by the couch, reliving the conversation I'd had with Allen just a half hour ago. The fire inside me, ignited by desperation and fury, burns so hot and bright that I know I won't let this go. Not even now.

"I told you, Ivy, we don't like to file a missing persons report until the person has been gone for twenty-four hours or more."

"Her car is still in the parking lot, Allen! What more do you—"

"And the doors were locked. There was no evidence of a struggle."

"It was snowing! Any tracks would have been covered. People don't just disappear, especially in Kennedy. The person who killed Vanessa has to be the one who took that girl."

"Who's the sheriff here?"

"It's supposed to be you. But we both know you have a knack for looking the other way. How's the investigation into Vanessa's murder going?"

"Watch it, Ivy."

It's too late, of course. That girl is dead. I grit my teeth and try to shove the image of her pink gloves out of my head. What could have happened to her? The question slams at the walls of my head.

A voice explodes from the voicemail, jerking me out of my reverie. Mom must have hit PLAY. Soon the entire message sounds throughout the trailer. Another company looking for payment. One we're late on, like all the others. Mom's knuckles turn white from her grip on the edge of the counter. I know I've only added to her burdens.

"I'm sorry."

The words are so inadequate, but they're all I have. Mom heaves a sigh and surprises me by stepping forward with outstretched arms. She smells like the diner and weariness and lavender. I hesitate for just an instant before wrapping my arms around her. I close my eyes and draw in a breath, savoring this. "I love you," I whisper.

Her hand cups the back of my head, as if I'm some small, innocent thing. "I love you too, kid."

For the first time in so long, it feels like the seconds finally slow down. I manage not to count them as they pass. Still, I'm the first one to pull away. "Why don't you go to bed?" I touch her cheek, the scar she's always had from the chicken pox. "I'll take care of some of these dishes."

She shakes her head. "No, I think I'll write for a while. But thanks, honey. You're sweet." The floor creaks—the music of my childhood—as she heads down the hall to her room. She has a tiny desk in there, next to Dad's pile of junk, where there's an ancient laptop and a fragile sense of hope in the air. Mom has wanted to be a writer since she picked up her first Danielle Steel book in 1972. *Star* was the book Mom got the damn parrot's name from. A tale of a woman's loss, strength, and accomplishment when her future seemed set in stone.

Just a few minutes later a familiar sound floats to my ears: tapping. Her fingers on the keys. My feet move of their own volition, and I find myself hovering in the doorway. I ignore the blue glow beneath Lorna's door and enjoy the sight of my mom, home and relaxing. She's changed out of her uniform and into a robe she's had as long as I can remember. The material is dotted with roses. There are holes in the elbows.

"Don't stay up too late, okay?" I say.

She doesn't respond; I know she can't hear me now.

Chapter Eight

Tap. Tap. Tap.

My first thought is that it's happened again. I'm sleep-walking, standing outside of Vanessa's trailer, shivering in the cold, some distant sound disrupting the stillness. But when my eyes open, I'm looking at the ceiling in my room instead of sky. When I was six I put plastic glow-in-the-dark stars above me. They lost their light a long time ago, but their shells remain, their idea, their memory. I blink, staring at the stars and hovering in the place between sleep and waking.

Tap. Tap. Tap.

The sound is so loud and close I jump. Not a dream. I fly upright, wild thoughts of killers and disappearing girls burning through my veins. Moonlight cascades across the floor, and instead of the square pattern of the glass, there's a long, man-shaped shadow. Slowly, forgetting how to breathe, I raise my gaze.

There's someone at my window.

Before I can scream, a familiar voice shout-whispers, "It's okay. It's just me."

"Myers?"

He doesn't disappear. That's when I know this is no delusion. I swing my legs to the side so fast that they tangle in the sheets and I fall. My cheeks are on fire as I free myself. I grab at the frame and pull. The window resists at first, but it's no match for my eagerness, disbelief, desperation.

A layer of frost covers the sill. Cold air creeps in as I lean out, blinking the sleep and ice from my eyes. It's been so long since he's been here, so close in proximity, that it takes me a moment to speak. "Um…hi." We haven't spoken in over three months. Why tonight? I tug at my boxer shorts—self-conscious even though he's seen every part of me—and try to smooth my hair into submission.

His hands are shoved in his pockets, and he's taken a step back. He looks so good in those jeans, that green coat. "Hi."

Silence. I don't know what to say. Neither does he, it seems. Eight seconds go by in a stiff, screaming hush. Words crowd in my mouth, things I can't release. *I still love you. I'm still so sorry. Don't move on. Forgive me.* Just like he forgave me every time he heard about something stupid I'd done or witnessed me risk the life I knew I wouldn't lose.

Finally I clear my throat. "What are you doing here?"

My ex-boyfriend's nose is turning red. His curls are askew, and I know that he came here from his bed. I imagine him tossing and turning as much as I have, and a warm feeling fills my stomach. Hope. No, I can't let myself hope. "…wanted to make sure you were okay," Myers is mumbling. He's back to avoiding my eyes. The seconds over those curls stare at me. Sixty-six years, two months, four days, thirteen hours, thirty-one minutes, and forty-one seconds. I imagine him as an old man, hauling armfuls of wood across the lumberyard. I want to picture myself there, too.

Instead, all I see is Ginger Marks.

"Are you and Ginger together now?" It just pops out, and I feel myself blanch.

Pause. Something in Myers's eyes flickers. "Yes."

It hurts. It hurts even more than I thought it would. "What do you mean, 'make sure you were okay'? Why wouldn't I be?" I ask in an impulsive attempt to change the subject.

"I was there tonight. At the diner. Everyone saw you go head to head with Allen."

This is where I would usually offer a lie. Tell everyone or anyone that I'm fine, I'm okay, I'm just tired or thinking. But Myers is different. From the beginning, he was always different. I swallow a sigh, wishing I were someone else, had more time, had been born without the numbers. Wishing that I could change the choices I made that summer night. "It's late, and you're going to get sick. Good night, Myers," I say. The words are broken and defeated. Laden with all the weight of the past three months. Suddenly Myers being here isn't wonderful, it's just painful. All those nights I cried myself to sleep, all the rebuffed attempts to repair what had been shattered.

I start to duck inside.

He stops me. "Ivy." When I lift my head to look at Myers again, trying to pretend my name on his lips doesn't affect me, he hesitates. Once again I count the seconds. *One. Two. Three. Four. Five.* "You gave up on me." Surprised, I jerk my gaze up to meet his. I don't know what I expected him to say, but it wasn't this. Myers doesn't ask why I stopped trying, if it can be called trying—there were only those phone calls in the beginning, those few attempts to approach him—but it floats between us anyway, a breath of air, an invisible ache.

I can't tell him about the dwindling days above my own head. I can't confide that it's better for him to stay mad at me. I can't make him see the absoluteness of the numbers.

It doesn't matter that he won't understand. It's the truth, the first one I've told since I can remember: "There wasn't enough time to fight for you."

He has no chance to respond.

I shut the window.

• • •

Russell Montgomery is eighty-one years old.

He lies in bed with his wrinkled hands folded over his chest. His eyelids, blue-veined and withered, are closed as he listens to my voice. I sit in the rocking chair beside him and push my foot against the floor to make it sway. The pages of his ancient poetry book crinkle as I turn them. "Oh, here's a good one," I say. "Dylan Thomas. 'Do not go gentle into that good night. Old age should burn and rave at close of day; Rage, rage against the dying of the light. Though wise men at their end know dark is right—'"

"You look tired."

I stop and smile at him. "How would you know?"

The old man makes an irritated sound in his throat. "Don't be a smartass."

My smile grows. His room is plain, bare. The walls around us are white, there are no rugs on the wooden floor. The curtains and his blanket are a matching blue, something the nurses probably put together. The only marks of individualism for the man are his books. They line a shelf opposite the bed, alphabetical and orderly. "Do you want me to keep reading?" I ask him, running my thumb along the edge of the paper.

His voice is a rumble in his chest. "I'd rather hear about what's bothering you."

I blink. "Nothing."

Russell *harrumph*s. "I'm old, girl, not stupid."

For the thousandth time I allow myself to wonder what it would feel like to tell someone. It's easy and impossible, terrible and wonderful. There have been so many times I've almost crumbled and confessed to the people closest to me. Mom, Vanessa, Myers. It always starts the same way. I look at them and wonder if they would believe me. I open my mouth…and then I close it again. The moment passes.

Just like this one. Because of course, in the end, I only give Russell a shadow for an answer. "I just wish things were different, that's all," I say.

The clock over the door ticks into the quiet. "My son was in a car accident when he was fifteen," Russell announces. He finally opens his eyes—they're a startling amber, a reflection of the young man he once was—and reaches for a picture frame on the nightstand. I hurry to take it from him. He settles back against his pillow as I glance at it. The image shows Russell, maybe thirty years ago, kneeling beside a man in a wheelchair. Those same amber eyes. His son. I don't even need to ask.

"He was paralyzed from the waist down," Russell tells me. "Back then, we didn't have the technology you have now. So he had to use the chair."

I've never been an eloquent person. All I come up with is: "Does he ever visit you?"

Another sound of impatience. "Of course he does. That's not the point."

I lean so far back in the rocking chair it creaks. I mark my place in the book with the tip of my finger. "What is the point, Russell?"

He adjusts his position in the bed, sitting up straighter. "The point is, my boy didn't waste time wishing things were different. He built up his upper body strength and did what he could. He worked on his grades instead of playing a sport. He still went out with his friends, he still had a job."

Didn't waste time. The old man doesn't know how appropriate it is. But we're venturing into dangerous territory; I don't want to think about all the things I don't have time to do. This place is about what I can do. "So you're saying I should start working out?" I ask lightly. Russell doesn't grace this with a response, and the silence stretches and thins. "Your son sounds like a strong person."

Feebly, he waves this away. "So are you, Miss Ivy. Now, why did you stop reading?"

At this, I roll my eyes—which he doesn't see because his are closed again—and find the poem. By the time he interrupts again, the hands on the clock are on the eight. "Aren't you going to be late for school, young lady?" he reminds me gruffly. The rocking chair hits the back of my legs as I stand. I say goodbye, bend, and kiss his pale cheek. He makes another disgruntled sound but pats my shoulder.

"You're a good girl. You're going to do great things."

It's the nicest thing anyone has ever said to me—I attempt one last smile for him before leaving. He doesn't notice, of course; he's lost in his own world, a simple place, I imagine.

As I pass Miranda's doorway, I peek in. She's sitting by the window, needlepoint forgotten in her lap. She gazes outside, unaware of the days only I can see. There's no time to talk to her. Rita waves as the front doors slide open and I walk into the gray morning.

I can never remember to put on gloves or a hat before leaving the house, so the tips of my fingers and nose darken and numb. On my way to the car I hug my elbows to me and imagine leaving here, going to some exotic, warm place. Anywhere away from here. A school bus blares by, and I hear kids laughing and shouting. I yank my hood up over my head and shiver, staring at my feet, the cracks in the pavement. Then I dig my keys out of my pocket, get in my car, and leave Hallett behind.

The school parking lot is full—finding a space takes too long. I'm late. But it turns out to be an advantage, because as soon as I step through the front doors, noise drowns out my thoughts. Locker doors slam and shouts bounce off the hallway walls. A little girl runs past, and as I get out of her way I slam into a warm, solid body.

"Sorry…" I start to say. The apology dies in my throat when I look up into Brent's familiar face.

His expression is unfathomable. His Adam's apple bobs

as he swallows, and he glances around as if to make sure no one sees us standing so close. "Look, Ivy, I wanted to—"

"Don't." The sound of his voice makes my insides turn to oil, and it forces me back to that night. *Hiding again?* Blue shadows. Pounding music. The glow of numbers casting a faint light over my skin.

My grip on the folders is so tight that the paper crinkles. "I'm late," I mumble around a tongue that feels like cotton. Brent doesn't try to stop me when I hurry away. But I feel his eyes on me until I turn a corner and disappear from sight.

Chapter Nine

"I need you to listen to me!"

Shannon Wyoming's voice bounces off the walls of the auditorium, and I can't hold back a cringe. Thankfully she can't see it; I stand at the far edge of the stage, half concealed by its red velvet curtain. The rest of the class is scattered in the plush seats facing the platform, and I note the glow of cell phones as some snap pictures of Shannon.

Thursday. Drama class. Auditions for parts in this semester's play.

"...never thought it would end this way," Shannon recites. But all I can hear is Vanessa's voice.

She was the one who made me sign up for this each semester. She had dreams of becoming the next Julia Roberts, and she was always the lead in the school play. She was Cinderella, Eliza Doolittle, Sandy. However, it didn't take long for our teacher, Mr. Weis—though everyone calls him Chuck—to realize that I didn't share her flair for the stage. Every time he tried to put me in front of a group, I froze. There was no sign of the recklessness that landed me in Allen's car or brought my mother to tears. So I've been filling his stagehand position for years and it's an arrangement we're both satisfied with.

This year Chuck is putting on a play he wrote himself. The title on the front of the script reads *On a Wednesday* in small black print. I'm just trying not to think about how perfect Vanessa would have been for this role. Shannon continues to strut back and forth with her lines in one hand, flourishing her other through the air as she speaks. No one has the courage to tell her how ridiculous she looks. Were it not for those shrinking numbers over her blonde head, I might. But Shannon is like a resident of Hallett—I want her ending to be a good one.

Despite how the sound of her voice makes me cringe.

Mitch Donovan stands beside her, looking bored. He's trying out for the male lead, of course. Grief hasn't deterred his determination to be the biggest and the best. He's always been like that, ever since we were little kids. Just another way he and Vanessa were alike.

"Okay, stop for a second."

Shannon glowers as Chuck gets up from his seat and ascends the small flight of stairs to her left. Our teacher is no small man, and with his beard and plaid shirts he seems more lumberjack than teacher. "You're doing great," he rumbles, "but this persona isn't quite right for Emily."

"I thought you said becoming a character is about personal vision," she argues, hand on her hip.

"To a point. But did Juliet laugh as she plunged the dagger into her heart? Did Heathcliff rejoice when he learned of Cathy's death? There are certain facades and reactions that are appropriate—expected—for a character, or a moment."

"So you're saying...I should be depressed?" Shannon questions with a frown. There's a tiny line between her eyebrows.

Chuck looks as if he's swallowed a bug. He opens the script, his large hands gripping it tightly. "Look at the lines, read them again," he urges. "Emily is *dying*. There's no hope, nothing left but goodbye. This is a story of resolutions, farewells, tying up loose ends. It's about the power of one person to change what she can in the little time she has left."

No one notices the way I take a step back, deeper into the shadows.

"I'd like to point out *yet again* that we're opening in December," Shannon says. "But I don't get how this is a Christmas play."

"It's not," Chuck replies shortly. Before Shannon can butcher the scene again, he scans the class. "Who's next? Ah...you! Yes, you! What's your name?"

The new girl slouches lower in the chair, as if she hopes it will swallow her. "Amanda Ryan," she mumbles. Shannon leaves the stage with a pout.

"Sorry, Amanda, I'm horrible with names. Will you come up here? Just read what I've underlined." Chuck walks to the side of the platform.

But the new girl doesn't move. "No, thanks."

"Well, she *should* audition," Shannon says to her friends, not bothering to lower that voice of hers. "She's got a real chance at getting the male lead."

As the girls around her laugh, I fix my gaze on Shannon.

"You're one to talk," I comment. "There's a lot of speculation about what exactly you get waxed at Jacqueline's salon. Someone mentioned seeing the word 'chest' on a receipt…"

"Was I talking to you?" she asks, glaring.

I glare right back and let myself ignore the numbers over her head for a few seconds. "You should do some soul-searching, Shannon. Maybe you'll actually find one."

Before she can respond, I turn my attention to the front again. Amanda and Chuck are still arguing. Our teacher's brow has lowered. "This class is primarily graded on participation, Miss Ryan. Just one scene will suffice for the week. All you need to do is try." Amanda hesitates, sees that he's not going to change his mind, and heaves herself to her feet. She takes her time getting to those stairs. I count the seconds as they pass. *One. Two. Three.* I remember the image of Amanda lying across the train tracks, looking up at the stars.

Once she reaches the center of the stage, Amanda just stands there, scowling. She's as tall as I am, and she tries to hide it by hunching over. *Four. Five. Six.*

"Go ahead," Chuck urges.

Amanda glares at her boots. *Seven. Eight. Nine.* She takes a soundless breath, and her black dreadlocks gleam. Everyone watches. Waits. I wonder if anyone else notices the way her hands tremble. *Ten. Eleven. Twelve.* It's at that moment I know she can't do it. One of us should come forward, volunteer.

"I'll do it," I hear someone saying.

It takes exactly three more seconds to realize it's me.

Maybe Chuck sees that he's not going to get anything out of Amanda. Or maybe he's just shocked that I want to audition for the first time in years. Whatever the reason, he shrugs his big shoulders in assent. Amanda bolts from the lights so quickly I wonder if she could have waited until the very last second to move from those tracks before the train came.

Even before I abandon the safety of the curtain, there are whispers. Now every stare turns to me. My insides quake, and somehow I'm walking to the place Amanda's just vacated. I squint. It's been so long since I've been here, in this spot. It feels strange. Wrong.

I can feel the heat of Mitch Donovan's hatred.

Slowly I turn to face him.

By some miracle, the lines stumble into my memory. "I need you to listen," I whisper, pain and fear crashing over me in a great wave.

Mitch doesn't seem to be aware of the way his fists clench. "Why should I?" he growls through his teeth. There are no lines for him yet; he's going off-script.

And something happens. Instead of a boy who's dumped milk on me, taught his friends to ostracize me, urged the town to despise me, I see another person. Someone else with the same red hair and burning blue eyes.

Vanessa's jaw works. She's wearing the pajamas she died in—those pink flowers are so fierce, so bright—and her skin is smeared with dirt and blood. It's even under her nails. Leaves cling to her hair.

There are no numbers hovering above her, because she has none left. She's dead.

There's a roar in my ears. I can't focus. I swallow, blinking at the words on the page. They're blurring and shaking and duplicating. I can't breathe. "I only have a few more weeks, at the most," I manage, "and I need to fix this before I go. I need to know that you don't hate me."

"It's too late for that," Vanessa says. Even her voice has changed. It's empty.

Somehow I manage to respond. "I know it's too late, I know that. But please. *Please*. Forgive me." Real pleading leaks into my voice.

My best friend doesn't even blink. "Fuck you…*Emily*."

It's the name that jars me. Suddenly I'm looking at Mitch again, we're holding lines in our hands, and there's an entire class watching us. I feel dazed, disoriented, as if I've stepped off a carousel that's been spinning too fast.

"That's enough, I think," Chuck says, clearing his throat. Normally he applauds improvisation, but this is different, and we all know it. "Great job, you two. Who's next?" Before the next contenders have even gotten up I'm fleeing back to my curtain, back to the darkness. Mitch leaps off the stage like he's completely unaffected by any of it. One of his friends gives him a high five when he sits.

Thud. Thud. Thud. Chuck's heavy footsteps behind me. Then his hand, hot and overwhelming, on my shoulder. "Are you all right?" he asks quietly. His voice makes me think of thunder.

No, I'm not all right. I'm a wound, raw and exposed and bleeding. "Why did you write this?" I ask him instead of giving him the lie I give everyone else. *I'm fine. Just fine. Of course. Why wouldn't I be?*

He doesn't blink, doesn't push me. "I wanted to imagine what it would be like, having a chance to say goodbye."

I utter a short, bitter laugh. I can feel the other kids

still staring, but for once, I don't care. "You say that like it's something so great."

My teacher's expression is thoughtful. I concentrate on his beard as he speaks rather than his pitying eyes. "Wouldn't it be, though?" he counters, as if this conversation isn't strange or out of place. "Knowing exactly how long you have? To talk to all those people you care about one last time, to make sure that they have everything they need to get closure?"

Why does everything come back to time? I bite my lip to hold in whatever sound is clawing its way up my throat. A scream or a sob, it doesn't matter. I want to tell Chuck that knowing when you're going to die doesn't make anything better, regardless of goodbyes or closure. That it can drive a person insane, if they let it. That having this knowledge isn't how things are supposed to be. We're all just meant to live in uncertainty, going through each day without the numbers telling us whether it's our last. The unknown is what makes us human.

Chuck stops waiting for me to give an answer. He turns to go. Before he leaves he murmurs, "By the way... you made a fantastic Emily."

I watch him walk away.

He has no idea that I *am* Emily.

• • •

Her picture finally appears in the paper.

She was twenty-two years old. A student. I scan the article, fragments standing out as if they're numbers. *Foul play is suspected. Authorities are saying there may be a link between Jill Briggs's disappearance and Vanessa Donovan's murder.*

Jill. Her name was Jill.

I cut it out and add it to my box.

Chapter Ten

Myers Patripski didn't know I existed until our sophomore year in high school.

Of course he knew who I was—everyone knows everyone in a place like Kennedy, and the notorious stories that spread about me and Vanessa certainly didn't help—but I felt invisible to him when we passed each other in the hallways. I saw him, though. Saw his brown eyes, his dimpled smile, his dark curls, the worn fabric of his shirts and the holes in his jeans. The sound of his laughter mesmerized me; it was rare but unrestrained.

Vanessa teased me endlessly about it. Myers Patripski was only a year older than us, but everyone knew he didn't date just anyone. He seemed so unattainable, and there always were my numbers to consider.

Yet the truth kept crackling inside of me, like sparks beneath the skin. I needed an outlet. Which is why, in a friendly slant of moonlight, I painted I LOVE MYERS

PATRIPSKI on a train car. It was my secret, my silent proc-lamation to the entire world. No one should have seen it.

But someone did. They took a picture and sent it out to the entire student body.

It didn't change anything, really. No one but Vanessa knew about my nighttime activities, so no one could have known it was my work. I walked through the halls and believed Myers still didn't see me. I didn't have the courage to tell him I did it, the words were mine.

So Vanessa told him.

I still remember the first words he ever spoke to me.

It was after classes, on a bright day. Vanessa was trying out for the cheerleading squad—kind of pointless, since our school is so small every girl gets a spot on the team—and I was sitting on the bleachers, picking at the loose skin around my nail. My fingers were stained blue and pink from the paint.

Sunlight streamed down on my bare legs and arms. Vanessa kicked her own tan limbs through the air, smiling so hugely that I could see her teeth even from the distance I was at. Only I knew that the beads of sweat glinting on her forehead might not be just from the heat. The coach blew her whistle, and the girls paused and gathered around. Some nodded. Vanessa just looked bored and tired. My skin was raw and bleeding now, so I absorbed myself in scratching the paint off as I continued to wait.

The bleachers began to tremble as someone walked over the rows. I glanced up when a shadow fell over me. "That was quick—" I started, adjusting my glasses.

Silence. My heart skipped a beat. I found myself

looking into Myers Patripski's serious eyes. Before I could croak a single word or some kind of comprehensible greeting—*Hello. I'm Ivy? You're amazing?*—he shoved his hands in his pockets and settled next to me. The bleachers shuddered again.

He didn't say anything at first. I stared straight ahead, concentrating on drawing air in and out of my lungs, and tried to think of something clever or casual. Something that would make me more than Ivy Erickson, the strange girl with one friend and a plain face and a sister who took her clothes off on the internet.

"I never know what to say," Myers announced abruptly.

I blinked. "What?"

He pursed his lips and gazed down at the tryouts. His expression was thoughtful, one I'd observed from afar many times before. And now he was talking to me, of all people. It was exhilarating and terrifying.

"When I see you at Nick's, or talking to your friend by the lockers, or going to your car, I always wish I was one of those guys who knew the right thing to say. The exact words that would start something, without it being obnoxious. You know? I'm not brave like you are."

My mind halted. Then it began to race. The blood quickened through my veins, too, fueled by wonder and disbelief. He'd noticed me? *When I see you.* Yes, he'd really said that. "I do know," I finally replied, amazed that there was no tremor in the statement.

He smiled. "Maybe I should have tried your method."

It took a moment for the words to register; I was too busy staring at the curve of his lips. "Wait. My method?" I frowned.

Myers raked his curls back, as if he were considering something. He pulled a cell phone out of his pocket. He moved his finger over the surface for a few seconds, mindless of the way I was admiring the slope of his cheekbones in the sunlight, then tilted the screen toward me.

When I saw the image, I stopped breathing altogether. Those beautiful-ugly-horrible-wonderful words taunted and stared back at me. I LOVE MYERS PATRIPSKI. He knew it was my work. He wouldn't be bringing it up if he didn't. "How…" I rasped. I stopped, cleared my throat. "Who told…" It occurred to me in that instant. Of course. No one else knew. For just a split second my fury clouded over the utter humiliation.

Vanessa.

Oh, she was dead. She was *dead*.

The coach blew the whistle again, and suddenly the girls were scattering. Vanessa grabbed her bag and bounded toward me, her hair a stream of fire. The bleachers quaked. She didn't even pause when she saw Myers.

He stood, and I noticed that he was smiling again. "See you around, Ivy," he murmured.

There was no chance to say goodbye, to explain or stumble over some lie or excuse for what I'd painted on the train car. He turned and made his way back toward solid ground, and Vanessa was already in front of me, blocking him from my sight, chattering animatedly about the uniforms. I craned my neck to get one last glimpse of him, but it was too late. I gave Vanessa a distracted response, and she tugged at me.

"I need some new sports bras," she announced, panting a little. "You're coming with me to Paula's."

I'd forgotten all about killing her, because I realized something as soon as Myers was gone. Like a shooting star illuminating the night sky.

I'd forgotten all about the numbers when I was with Myers Patripski.

• • •

The clear sound of a bell vibrates through the diner. "Order up!" Amar calls, returning to the fryer. His favorite music fills the kitchen, clashing with the country tunes Nick has on for our customers. I asked Amar to translate one of his songs for me once. It didn't make any more sense in English.

Steam rises from the hot water in front of me. I bend over the sink, a bead of sweat sliding down my brow, and scrub vigorously at a pot. Mom hurries up to the counter and snatches two more of the plates. She winks at me, a wisp of hair clinging to her eye from the static, and whisks the food away. It's busy tonight; every table is full. Earlier I saw kids from school, two of my teachers, the manager of the Kennedy co-op, Ray, the McCorks, the mayor, the florist, and Dr. Simonson. Mom and Susie are mint-green blurs on the floor. At least she'll make enough in tips to pay the electric bill this month.

Suddenly there's a commotion by the front door. Another group of kids from school is walking in, and someone is shouting. Amar pauses, spatula in hand. I leave the sink to peer around the corner. There's a flurry of elbows, and then Brent is being shoved toward the wall. "Just calm down, man!" he urges, glancing in his parents' direction. Then he spots me, and his eyes widen.

"*Where is she?*"

It takes me a moment to see Mitch Donovan. But then he's all anyone can see as he storms past the booths and around the counter. His clothing is wrinkled, as if he just woke up, and his red hair is a nest. I can smell the alcohol from yards away. Mitch veers abruptly, barging toward the kitchen.

Uncle Nick appears like some sort of apparition, blocking Mitch's way. "Staff only," he states. The top of his head glints where he's going bald. There's something in his voice I've never heard before.

Shock renders me unable to move, hide, run. Mitch's wild, red-rimmed eyes focus on me. He grapples at Uncle Nick's shoulder, trying to get by him. My uncle is a tree, firmly rooted in the doorway. "You knew she needed you!" Mitch screams, pointing his finger at me.

Brent is back, jerking Mitch away, and Allen McCork is on his other side. Together they manage to put some distance between us. Allen mutters something in Mitch's ear, but whatever he says doesn't calm him. "Who are you protecting?" Mitch shouts. The diner has gone deathly silent. Everyone in Kennedy will hear about this spectacle by tomorrow.

The bell over the door jangles as they leave, and it's over. But Mom's grip is tight on my elbow. Uncle Nick has his arm wrapped around my shoulders. Amar stands behind me. Susie is beside him. They hold and surround me like a shell around a yolk, as if they expect me to break.

"Don't listen to him, honey," Mom hisses. "Don't you dare."

"He's an idiot," Amar agrees.

"He's never coming back in here again, that's for sure," Uncle Nick says. He sounds more normal now.

Their words barely penetrate; I'm staring out the window, into the night and the black depths of the trees.

My mind, desperate for a distraction or foothold, works quickly. There's nothing beyond the woods, in front or behind Nick's. The windows face the road. The night she disappeared, Jill was the only stranger to stop here. She was inside for a just few minutes, but it was long enough for someone to notice her.

I'm such an idiot. How did I not see it before?

It's so obvious. Something that I shouldn't have missed. Something the sheriff had to have already concluded.

The killer was in the diner that night.

Chapter Eleven

REWARD.

Jill's smiling face adorns Hallett's front door. Below the grainy photograph it reads, *$10,000 reward for any information leading to the whereabouts of Jill Briggs.* They're all over town. I avoid her gaze as I pull the door open and slip inside. Rita waves when I pause to loosen the scarf around my neck. I give her a distracted smile in return and head for a resident I haven't visited in a while.

Eunice Hastings.

She has more wrinkles than any other person I've seen, and she's lost every tooth but one. The moment I'm in her room the smell hits me—rotting food. No matter how often the staff cleans the walls and the floor, they can't seem to get everything that Eunice throws at them during her mealtimes. I still remember one morning, when they gave her oatmeal. She dipped the tips of her old fingers into the mush and chucked it at me. *Here, want some? Take it, have some!*

The old woman has two years, one month, nine days, fourteen hours, ten minutes, and fifty-eight seconds left to torment Hallett.

The moment I enter, her head snaps up and her gaze narrows. "Oh, it's you," Eunice says in her high voice. It's surprisingly clear and unwavering, despite how breakable she looks. "I thought it was that stupid boy who brought me yogurt. The stuff was tasteless! Tasteless!" She's so frail and vicious that the staff lets her stay in bed most of the time. Her hair is cropped short so they don't have to wash it every day.

Settling into the chair by the window, I nod with supposed sympathy. "Yogurt isn't my favorite, either."

Now Eunice squints at me, suspicion in the thin line of her lips. Her eyes are bright. "Why do you keep coming back? I told you to leave me alone! I just want to be left alone!"

It's something she's said before, and often. Unperturbed, I hug my knees to my chest and feel the frost on the glass against my elbow. "Why do you hate the world, Eunice?"

She scowls. "The world hates me. It does, it does. Hates me. Unfair, cruel, stupid world."

The words bring me back. A few weeks ago, I abandoned my will to go on. It was after the breakup with Myers, after Vanessa's murder. My numbers were ticking down, getting closer and closer to the last one. I locked myself in my room and stared at the glowing digits in the mirror's reflection. No lights, no music. Just the sound of my breathing and the isolating knowledge of my own imminent death.

Then I thought of Eunice, remembered those words.

The old woman doesn't know it, but she was the one who made me want to be strong. Because I didn't want to use my time lamenting the cruel world. Or mourning the quality of food. I didn't want to be her.

So I got up and turned on the light.

And here I am. Eunice rants and rages about a variety of trivialities over the next hour. Her ungrateful children, the awful cold, the pain in her wrists. I make sounds of agreement and just listen. Sometimes that's all a person needs, really. To be heard. But then the clock is warning me that school is starting soon, I need to go.

I stand. "See you soon, Eunice," I say. She swears at me, and since she has no food to throw, spits in my direction. The glob lands at my feet. I leave to the sound of her shrieking obscenities. It echoes down the hall, and a nurse is heading this way. She sees me and rolls her eyes.

I avoid looking at Jill's poster as I leave. The fall air teases my senses, and I take a deep breath, digging for my keys. The trees are brown now. Soon they'll be completely bare, then covered in white. I won't be around to see them go back to green.

The thought causes my stomach to knot. As I turn away, I notice a man sitting on the bench just outside the front doors. He has tousled gray hair and drooping eyes, like the elephant I painted on Friday. I start to walk past him, heading for my car, but his voice stops me: "Are you Ivy Erickson?"

Fear lodges in my throat. I face the man, appraising him again. He's not from around here, that I know. The glowing numbers over him count down from thirty-five years, seven months, ten days, eleven hours, forty-two minutes, and two seconds. "Yes, I'm Ivy," I answer after a pause that's too long.

He extends his hand to me. The sleeve of his black coat is so long it nearly hides his fingers. "I'm Paul Briggs," he says.

I frown now, looking into those gray eyes again. Why is the name so familiar?

"Jill's father." His voice catches. He makes a visible effort to regain his composure. "The sheriff told me you'd probably be here."

Jill's father. I take a step back, my breath catching. I didn't want to think about the girl with the pink gloves having a father. Fresh guilt surges through me. "What do you...I mean, how can I—"

Paul clears his throat. "The sheriff said you were the last one to see her."

I don't know what he expects from me; Allen probably knows more than I do about Jill's disappearance. But I still nod and say, "Yeah, I was." Her voice sounds in my head again. Sweet. Worried. Frustrated. I see her numbers, so white and small. Twenty-two minutes. So much can happen in twenty-two minutes. A person can get a cup of coffee. Have a conversation. Disappear from a parking lot.

"...just want to know what she said," Paul is saying. There's a defeated note in the words. "What her last moments were like."

Jill's father has lost hope. I can see it. He knows what I do: she's gone. I want to give him this, I want to find some kind of comfort where there is none. For a few seconds I fumble for the right words. "She was nice," I tell him lamely. "Her car wasn't working, so I offered to get our mechanic to look at it for her. She thanked me."

I don't know what else there is. As the quiet lingers, Paul looks at the pink horizon and nods. His lips purse to hide the way they tremble. I bite my own, wishing I had more.

Suddenly I hear myself saying, "I'm going to find out what happened to her, Mr. Briggs. I promise."

He doesn't believe me. It's obvious in his smile. "Thank you, Ivy," he murmurs. "It was nice to meet you."

I don't respond. He's already walking away, hunched against the cold. He unlocks the door of a silver car and gets inside. I'm still standing in the middle of the lot as he reverses, then drives away.

What are you doing? the wind asks. *Go to school.* But I still don't move. My attention goes back to those trees. Resolve hardens in the pit of my stomach, replacing the fear, the pain. I may not see spring, but before the winter is finished, I will find Vanessa and Jill's killer. If not for them, or for me, for people like Paul Briggs.

Even if it's the last thing I ever do.

Chapter Twelve

Uncle Nick never throws away his receipts. If the police took them for the investigation, he'll have copies. My uncle cherishes his family, but we're nothing compared to his diner. Uncle Nick even makes us print receipts for the cash payments and write names on them. Information on each of the customers we served the night Jill disappeared is in his office. It's only a matter of slipping inside when he's not around—he wouldn't let me look at them if he knew the reason why.

After school I hurry to work. The bell rings as I shove the door open. Tonight the air smells like fish. "Hi, darlin'," Susie drawls, chewing on her usual wad of gum. She's pouring one of Allen's deputies a pot of coffee, and her hair is blue; her dye jobs often go wrong. Mom is talking to Amar, nodding as he reviews new items on the menu. Neither of them notices me come in.

I make a beeline for the office, holding my breath. There Uncle Nick sits, his head bent, pen in hand. When

I come in he's scribbling something. At the sound of my entrance, he looks up. "How was school?" he asks, just like every other day. His pale eyes—my eyes—are worried. Since Mitch's outburst, my diner family has been on edge.

It's a good thing I've become an adequate liar.

"Long," I answer, my heart pounding at the sight of his desk. The safe is for cash, the drawers are for receipts. I learned this a long time ago, when I played in here once and decided to open those drawers, discovered the small slips of paper, and tore them into confetti. It was the first and only time my uncle had ever yelled at me. I still remember the way his ruddy skin darkened and how the veins bulged in his neck and forehead. Uncle Nick never gets angry. As a rule, he's the calmest person I know.

"Busy tonight?" I hang up my jacket.

"Steady. Not crazy."

Once I'm clocked in, I tie my apron, tossing him a smile before heading to the kitchen. I grab the bin and go onto the floor to take the dirty dishes back.

Hours pass, marked by the clock above the doorway and the numbers over Amar's hairnet. Uncle Nick never makes an appearance. He usually does once or twice a night, to talk to the regulars. I frown impatiently, taking my frustration out on an already-clean plate. Water sloshes against the rim of the sink. Why isn't he leaving the office?

"Order up!" Amar shouts.

"Honey, would you mind cleaning up the big corner booth?" Mom asks, coming to take the steaming plates. "Pastor Bob brought the family tonight. They made a mess."

She doesn't wait for me to answer. I drop the scrub brush and walk into the dining area, bin in hand again. It's not so busy anymore and I scan the faces that are here. My gaze lands on Amanda Ryan, sitting by herself in a small corner booth. I glance over my shoulder, toward the office. The door is still cracked open, light pouring out onto the floor. He hasn't left. I turn back to Amanda and an idea blooms. Without hesitation, I approach. She's not reading or texting like the other loners. She's just eating, gazing out the window. She looks like she's finally showered, though her clothing is horribly wrinkled. "I need you to do me a favor," I say without preamble.

Amanda doesn't jump. She just dips a fry into a blob of ketchup, looking bored. The movement causes the sleeve of her shirt to pull up slightly, and I see the angry red of newly healed cuts. "Why should I do you any favors?"

It takes me a moment to respond. "Maybe because I saved you from complete humiliation during our drama class the other day."

The new girl pauses at this, scowling. Part of the fry has lodged between her front teeth. "What do you want, then?" she snaps.

I grip the bin tighter, making the plastic creak, and lower my voice. "I want you to distract my uncle. Demand to see him."

"And say what?"

"I don't care. Complain about the thermostat, your burger, whatever. Just keep him out here for ten minutes, at least."

Amanda sits back, sighing. Her bangs fly up, then slowly settle haphazardly back into her eyes. "Do I dare ask why?"

Mom is glaring at me. I wave at her before facing

Amanda again. "No, you don't," I say shortly. "Are you going to help me or what?"

Her seconds tick down. I watch them, feeling my jaw clench. *Eleven. Ten. Nine. Eight.* "Fine," Amanda growls. "Five minutes. That's it."

Some of the tension eases out of my muscles. "Thank you."

"Don't thank me; after this we're even. Got it?"

"Got it." Before she can change her mind, I hasten to the table Pastor Bob's family was at. It takes a few minutes to clear the food-crusted plates and silverware. They must have brought the baby, too, because there's a mess on the floor. The next time I look in Amanda's direction, Uncle Nick is lumbering toward her. I hope she's not as bad here as she was in class. I can tell my uncle hasn't had a smoke in a while; he's twitching again.

Five minutes.

Amar says something to me when I dump all the bin's contents into the sink. The music is too loud to make out the words. I nod at him, hoping it's the right response. Amar focuses on the stove again. I don't waste time; I slip back out into the hallway and into the office. No one sees me. I shut the door just in case.

It feels strange to sit in Uncle Nick's chair. There are grooves in the cushion from his legs. I never realized how much smaller I am than him.

Never mind that! I stoop and check each drawer. They all hold small boxes—recipe boxes—and each one has months' worth of receipts in it. What was the exact date Jill was taken? My nails dig into my palm while I think. October 22nd. Yes, that's it. I open a few until I find the right box, then pull the tabs forward, looking for the day. It's near the front. I scan the names, some printed clearly, others near-intelligible scribbles. My palms are sweating. Ray Carson. Allen McCork. Kim Nash. Carl Blue.

Then one of the names stands out like a neon sign. *Myers Patripski.* His spot at the booth, empty. Exactly when Jill disappeared. The memory has been hovering in the back of my mind because I've been so upset he was there with Ginger. He could have slipped out the back door.

Denial instantly rises. No, it wasn't him. I laugh a little. I'm so desperate to find the killer that I'm suspecting anyone. Even my ex-boyfriend. *Get a grip, Ivy.*

I'm still smiling when my gaze lands on the name scrawled across the next receipt. The smile slowly dies. *Mitch Donovan.*

Once again, I think back to that night. I never saw him. Not once. He couldn't have stayed long. I think of his drunken accusation, his glares, his cruelties at school. Out of all the people that think I'm hiding something, he's always been the loudest. The angriest. A memory flashes before me, an image of Vanessa evading his grasp at her party. Maybe his rage is covering something else.

Guilt.

Chapter Thirteen

Dust motes float through the air. Rather than try to pay attention to the talk that hums all around me, I count the glowing fragments. One. Eleven. Thirty-three. I sit in a desk at the back, also ignoring the bright glow of everyone's timers.

"Come on, you guys!" Ms. Hanson urges, her voice bouncing off the walls, forcing me to listen now. "This is called a *group* discussion. Let's pay attention and engage. So Lennie is ashamed he killed the puppy, right? After all, he tries to hide it. But why would he be so afraid of George finding out? Hasn't George seen Lennie at his worst already?" Silence greets her.

I've lost count of the dust motes.

One of the football players finally speaks up. "Because the guy has tantrums," he drones.

No, that's not why. But I still don't answer. More ideas are muttered or suggested. *He likes dogs a lot. He doesn't want anyone to know how strong Lennie is.* None of them have any idea what it means, what it feels like to have someone and know that he is slipping through your fingers. Finally, I can't stop myself from muttering, "It's because he loves him." The statement is quiet—I don't even mean to speak out loud—but our teacher still hears.

"Interesting thought, Ivy. Why should Lennie's affection for George make him feel ashamed, rather than being able to tell him the truth?"

I feel as if I'm drowning. I lift my head and meet Ms. Hanson's encouraging gaze. "It doesn't matter that George loves him, too," I tell her. "It doesn't matter that a friend should be able to accept someone—Lennie—flaws and all. He's different, and he's done something no one will understand."

Amanda, who never speaks during class, says, "It's not like he could help it." She sits in the opposite corner from me. Her hood is drawn up so I can't see her face.

"That doesn't matter," I counter. "It's still horrible. Normal people won't accept it."

Someone coughs to disguise laughter. All of them think my passion is strange, that my sudden vehemence is embarrassing. And it is. I try to shrink inside myself. Ms. Hanson is talking again, but her voice has returned to its distant hum. To stay occupied, I pick up my pencil and draw a star on the corner of my notebook. I remember astronomy class, when we talked about how a star dies. Some go quietly, some explode.

The bell rings, and I'm one of the first out the door.

Amanda catches up with me after class. "You were pretty intense for a discussion about an old book," she comments.

She's waiting for me to respond. I shrug, adjusting my

books. "Yeah, well. I take everything seriously. Even when I don't want to."

"Why?"

I don't answer because my throat has suddenly gone tight—it always does in this hallway. This was Vanessa's domain, where she kissed Brent goodbye and looped her arm through mine as we went to class. This is where her locker still is. But it's not just a locker anymore.

It started with a paper heart. Someone cut it out with such painstaking detail, then taped it to Vanessa's locker. Someone else left her a note, just a few sloppy lines telling her how much she's missed. Then others noticed and wanted to do something. Now there are pictures, quotes written on the metal door in black marker. Nothing from me, though.

My pace quickens. If Amanda notices anything amiss, she doesn't comment this time. She just walks alongside me.

We've reached my locker. Remembering her question, I turn and look Amanda in the eye. It's strange, but I find myself resenting her for that night in the depot. Seeing Vanessa's shrine has stripped away my careful facades. She wants to know why I take everything seriously? "Because even when some of us stay away from train tracks, we're running out of time," I hiss. I catch one of Shannon's friends openly staring at me. I'm so, so tempted to put my foot out and trip her—she won't die, not until she's eighty-nine—but I resist. The last thing I need is another trip to the principal's office.

The new girl says nothing as I enter my combination, drop my old books inside, take out the ones I need next, and slam the locker door shut again. Still she doesn't reply.

But I feel her watching me as I walk away.

. . .

Mitch Donovan is throwing a Halloween party.

Amanda Ryan is old news now. All anyone wants to talk about lately is the costume they're going to wear. No one seems to think it's strange that Mitch is throwing a party just months after his twin's death. But then, he was once known for his parties, and everyone is slowly forgetting about Vanessa. Maybe it's not so odd, really. They're all looking forward while I'm forever reliving the past.

For once I pay attention to the chatter—the party might be the opportunity I need to find out more about Mitch. I can search his room, maybe even talk to him. The best thing about a costume party is that a mask is all it takes to become another person.

I head for Hallett after school. The route always takes me right through town. I pass the antique store, the general store, the gas station, Ray's shop, Paula's clothing store. Everything is normal, like every other day in Kennedy. But as I pass the clinic, my heart leaps. Suddenly my foot has a mind of its own and the car stops as it presses down on the brake.

Myers.

He's standing on the sidewalk with Ginger, and they look like they're arguing. Neither of them notices me in the middle of the road. Ginger shakes her head, her expression tight and angry. Myers rubs the back of his neck in the way he always does when he's frustrated. Then Ginger abruptly swings around, digging around in her purse. Keys flash; she must have finished her shift in the clinic cafeteria. Myers calls after her, and she says something back but doesn't turn around.

He continues to stand there. Daylight is bleeding away, and orange leaks across the skyline.

Mustering what bravery I have left, I roll my window down. "Need a ride?" I call hesitantly.

Myers jumps. He turns and spots me. Where once he would smile—a sly curve of the lips that made me feel as if the two of us shared a secret no one else in the world knew—now there's only the way his eyes darken. A muscle in his jaw flexes. He glances around, probably hoping another option will present itself. When it doesn't, he steps off the sidewalk and opens the door to my car. He gets in without saying anything.

Wordlessly, I pull forward. The only stoplight in Kennedy—right in front of us—is green, so there are no more pauses on the way out of town. I pass Hallett and Main Street turns into County Road 7. Myers lives ten miles into the country. He hasn't told me to go anywhere else, so the assumption is safe, I think.

I'm holding my breath and my knuckles are white on the steering wheel. I hadn't realized how much I miss his cologne. Its scent has long since faded on the only sweater of his I still have. It's buried in my closet, where I can find it during my weak moments. I glance over at him, looking at his worn sneakers, his jeans, his parka, his disheveled curls and stormy eyes. His hands are fists on his knees, but it's easy to recall how long his fingers are, how capable.

I focus on the road again, clearing my throat. "How are things at the yard?"

"The same," he answers flatly. "It never changes."

Desperately I try to keep him talking. "I heard Mike is going to promote you, when Fred retires."

"That's what they tell me." His head is turned, and he watches the dismal landscape dart by. A storm is coming.

I wipe one a damp palm off on my thigh while he's not looking and put it back on the steering wheel. "Well… that's exciting."

Myers makes a sound in his throat. Suddenly I can feel the heat of his attention, and I'm the one absorbed by the scenery. "We don't have to do this," he says, the words cold and hard as diamonds.

"Do what?" I ask, though my heart is sinking.

"The small talk. The pretending. There's nothing wrong with silence."

Finally our eyes meet. Three seconds pass. Softly I say, "Yes, there is."

My ex-boyfriend looks away first. "How is Lorna?" he asks now. I wince. He knows it's a sore spot for me, people asking about my sister—they only do because they watch her show. They want to make a point. We're worthless. We're trash. And yet they're the ones logging on.

I push the blinker down and take a left. "I thought you stopped hating me," I remark after a long pause.

He frowns. "What?"

"That night you came to my house. You were different, like you used to be. I thought—"

"You thought wrong, Ivy," Myers growls. The cab of my small car is hot, too hot. "I had a moment of weakness. It had been a bad day, and you…" He doesn't finish.

I try to sound strong. Accepting. I'm glad I'm driving, though, so he doesn't see the bright sheen to my eyes. "Fine. I get it. You'll never forgive me. That's okay."

Somehow, my calm seems to make him angrier. "How? How is that okay, Ivy?" Myers demands. He's leaning closer, and I can't concentrate. The lines of the road blur. I feel as if he wants to shake me and kiss me all at once. I can't deny that I want him to. Either touch, any response. Just to feel his skin on mine again.

Then I find an anchor. My gaze flicks to the rear view mirror, and my own numbers smirk back. One month, twenty days, nine hours, seven minutes, and thirty-three seconds. My racing heart begins its return to normal. "It just makes things easier, is all," I breathe.

Myers stares at me. Then he seems to deflate, facing the window again. "I'd forgotten how confusing you are sometimes," he mutters at the roiling sky.

I can't stop myself from saying, "I haven't forgotten anything." The words sound so fragile, things Myers can stomp on and shatter if he chooses to.

But he doesn't. He doesn't utter a word. The miles and the trees go by. We're close to the house when Myers finally breaks the silence. "You take a left up—"

"I remember where it is."

His jaw works. "Right." The gravel of his driveway crunches beneath the tires. Already I can hear the dogs barking. The waning canopy of leaves casts shadows over us, and soon the house appears up ahead. I haven't been here in so long, and a nostalgic pang fills my throat. The same wood siding, the same porch swing. Their two golden labs come sprinting over, and their tails whack the side of my car.

Myers quickly gets out. "Thanks for the ride," he says without turning.

I don't look at him, either. Instead, I keep gazing up at his house, wondering if his sisters are watching us through those wide windows. They probably hate me, too. "You're welcome."

He surprises me when he doesn't immediately leave. Instead, Myers lingers with one hand on the door. The wind increases as the storm draws closer. The dogs reappear and sniff around his ankles. For a moment it seems like he wants to say something—something different, without the barbs or the poison—but eventually he just shuts the door and walks away.

"I love you," I whisper, knowing he can't hear. *I'll always love you.*

Until the day I die.

Chapter Fourteen

It's raining on the night of Mitch's party.

Just a light drizzle, but it's enough to make my hair spring free of its bun. I almost miss the snow. This is Minnesota weather; it can never seem to decide if it's still fall or officially winter. I'm nervous as I walk up the front steps. The Donovans' not-so-new house is an old farmstead. They were only able to afford it because it was abandoned and run-down, but I don't blame them for not wanting to live in their old trailer anymore. Though she's gone, it still feels as though Vanessa lives there. It looks like they've done some work since I last saw this place. A fresh coat of paint, slabs of wood to replace the rotting ones on the porch.

Multicolored lights pulse through the windows and music makes the ground vibrate. Kids are everywhere. There's a huge crowd on the porch, some sitting on the rails, some standing around and shouting to be heard over the deafening beat. Tendrils of cigarette smoke curl through the air. Pumpkins line the stairs, lit from within by flickering candles. Fake cobwebs stretch across the railings.

Everyone is in costume.

There's Abraham Lincoln, a taco, a doctor. I recognize some faces and others are too concealed. There's so much going on that no one seems to notice me fighting toward the front door. I wonder where Mitch's parents are. They must be out of town; since Vanessa, the Donovans haven't exactly been social. They probably wouldn't approve of this. In fact, I know they wouldn't—I can see a keg through the dining room window.

As I brush past a girl in a cat outfit, I clutch at my own dress as if it's a lifeline. I'm wearing one of Lorna's Halloween getups. I think it's meant to be the black swan, though I've never really heard the story. It's a sleeveless thing, with a deep *V* for a neckline, and the bodice is stiff dark lace. The skirt is full and rustles with every movement. The matching mask on my face covers everything from my forehead to just above my lips. It's one of the few times I've put in my contacts, and they feel strange.

Since I loathe heels, I'm wearing black sneakers.

As soon as I step inside I slam into someone hidden behind a werewolf mask. "Sorry," I mutter. The wolf doesn't respond before he hurries away. He must be from the basketball team, he's so tall.

The air reeks of beer and sweat. Everyone from school is here. The living room is full of writhing bodies dancing to the roar of the stereo, the dining room is trashed with plastic cups and pizza boxes, and the hallway is dark and hot with couples snatching a few moments together. I don't see Mitch anywhere. There's Shannon, dressed as a princess.

She's sitting on the bottom stair and is clearly on her way to becoming drunk. "…always wanted to learn how to play the harmonica," I hear her slur to someone as I step past.

There are only three rooms upstairs. One of them is a bathroom. The other, I see when I poke my head in, is a storage room. This would have been Vanessa's.

I keep going.

My heartbeat thundering in my ears, I push the last door open. The hinges let out a long whine. It's too dark. I reach for the light switch and blink rapidly as my vision adjusts. It's Mitch's—there are posters for rock bands on the wall. The bed in the corner is unmade and clothes litter the floor. There's a distinct smell of cologne, as if he just sprayed it.

Mitch could come up here any second, so I don't waste time. His desk is covered with what looks like unfinished homework, a pack of gum, a lamp, textbooks. I yank the small drawers open. Pens. More notebooks. His porn stash.

There has to be something here. My fingers tremble as I comb through the magazines, hoping he's hidden something within the pages. I don't know what I'm looking for, exactly, but I can't deny anymore that I want the killer to be Mitch. I want answers to all the unanswered questions, a solution to the awful mystery, justification for the way he seeks to blame me for everything. Yes, it's unimaginable that he would kill his sister—my best friend—but at least the not knowing would no longer haunt me all day, every day, each second.

Suddenly the floor behind me creaks. "What are you doing?"

I let out a shriek, yanking the bottom drawer clear out

of the desk. Papers flutter down and scatter. Then I see who it is. "*Myers*," I exhale. Relief is so staggering that I flatten my hand on the desk for support.

"What are you doing?" he repeats, more forcefully this time. His glance flicks to the mess I've made. His expression is strange.

Probably because he's just caught you digging through someone else's things. Sense creeps back and I frown. I try to come up with an excuse, any excuse, for what I'm obviously doing. But there's nothing. "H-how did you know it was me?"

"Your hair isn't exactly subtle, Ivy," he says. The words aren't meant to sting, oddly enough. Though his tone is exasperated, there's a hint of wistfulness.

Swallowing, I choose that moment to notice what he's wearing. Myers isn't the type to ever wear a costume, but Ginger must have convinced him to dress up, since he's got a white button-up on, along with black slacks. There's something in his right pocket. A mask? Regardless, he looks good. *And he's still waiting for you to answer*, that voice in my head nudges. I swallow again, squatting to rake up the papers and put them back in the drawer. "I was just…I was…"

Myers steps closer. The tips of his shoes appear in front of me, gleaming in the light. I try to focus on what I'm doing. "Did you know you're a terrible liar? I think I told you a few times when we were together," he comments.

When we were together. The words coming out of his mouth are painful and exhilarating. So that time wasn't a dream, a fantasy. Somehow, hearing the affirmation from him makes it harder.

After I've fit the drawer back into space, I make a vague gesture, hoping Myers won't press this. "I'm looking for something."

"Obviously. What is it?"

"I-I don't really know." Myers just raises his brows at me. "You don't want to hear this, do you? Why are you still here? Look, I'll go. I'll stop. It was stupid anyway." I start to leave, but he's still in my way.

And he isn't moving. "Ivy," he growls. It's hard to breathe when he says my name, and I hope he doesn't notice. "What was stupid?"

"Move."

"No."

To avoid looking into his eyes, my glance goes higher. His timer marks the seconds. *One. Two. Three.* This dress is too tight. Panic and need rises inside of me. Unstoppable, uncontrollable. Memories that I've locked away spring free. The rumble of my father's voice. Vanessa's missing front tooth when we were six. The sound of my mother's typing. The muffled sobs behind my sister's door. Myers's soft smile as we faced each other on his bed. Then a door closing, open and unseeing eyes, a laptop slamming shut, music echoing through the trailer, a phone ringing and ringing and ringing in my ear. Numbers. So many numbers.

This time the chaos inside won't be silenced, and it comes out of me in a burst of passion that shocks both of us. "Everyone thinks the person who killed Vanessa is the same one who took Jill. Even Allen thinks so!" I snap at Myers. There's a crash downstairs, and a smattering of laughter. We ignore it. "Both young girls, both redheads," I continue. "Whoever it is was in the diner that night, and

I've gone through all the customers. The only one that stood out to me as a possibility was Mitch."

"Are you kidding, Ivy?"

"Why does he hate me more than everyone else? Where did he go after he left the diner? And you want to know what his alibi is for the night she died? He was supposedly off shooting bottle rockets with a of couple guys from the team. They could easily be covering for him."

He shakes his head, and even though he's so close I could touch him, he's never been more far away. "Are you hearing yourself right now? Look, I know losing Vanessa like that has to be devastating." The word makes him wince. "But her brother isn't a murderer, okay?"

I can't let go, give up. Not when Paul Briggs is putting up posters all over town and Vanessa's file has an UNSOLVED stamp across it in glaring red letters. "It was someone in the diner that night, Myers," I insist. "I went through the receipts, and no one else had a reason—"

The floor creaks out in the hallway.

We both freeze. My glance darts to the doorway, but there's no one. Just lights and noise. "Someone was listening," I realize, my stomach lurching.

Myers lets out a breath. "Ivy, you need to calm down."

This infuriates me. Everything else I've been keeping inside surges to the surface, wanting up, out. I fight it and lose. "You don't know!" I say through my teeth. "You don't know what I've had to endure these last months. Knowing what I know, then losing everyone. Vanessa, you. It's too much. I can't...I can't..." I press the heels of my hands to my eyes.

He isn't annoyed now. I can feel the heat emanating from Myers's body as he comes closer.

His palm cups my elbow, and I struggle with another rush of pain and longing. "Let go of me!" I cry, jerking away. The music slows downstairs. I shudder and reach beneath the mask to swipe angrily at the traitorous tears, keeping my back to him. "I can't bear to have you touch me. Not when you're with *her*." Never have I said anything with such venom.

Silence. Then Myers asks quietly, "What can I do?"

I face him again, my insides hardening. I wish I could hide how much of an effect he still has on me. "You can leave me alone," I answer.

"Ivy?" He dares to touch me again, on my bare shoulder.

It's been so long since I've felt his skin against mine. That familiar current of electricity travels through me. He feels it too. Before he can make an excuse that will cut, or take the step back that will burn, I do it. "You're right; this was crazy. Mitch isn't a killer. I'm sorry. Just forget this. Forget all of it."

I turn away, my gaze glued to the floor, and that's when I see them.

The world shrinks. The music becomes white noise.

They must have fallen out of the drawer when I pulled it out. Somehow I missed it. They lie there silently pleading.

A pair of pink gloves.

Maybe some part of me didn't really believe it, that Mitch is the one behind the murders. Why else would those gloves be here, though? The last time I saw them they were on Jill Briggs's hands. My mind races. What should I do? Take them? Leave them for the sheriff's office to find?

But Allen won't listen if the information comes from me. The last time I made a tip I wound up a suspect.

A metallic taste abruptly fills my mouth and everything tilts. I run into the hall, and the music assaults me again. I think Myers says my name, but it's too loud. I might have imagined it.

Someone swears in my ear as I shove past. Throat dry, too dry. I look for something to drink besides alcohol, but all I see is beer cans and bottles with amber liquid sloshing around inside. On my way to the kitchen, though, I pause. Two girls are staring up at the family portrait on the wall. Part of me wants to keep running, but part of me wants to hear their thoughts, what they knew about her. My best friend. Her memory quiets the inner chaos that finding the gloves in Mitch's room has caused.

"She was only seventeen," one of the girls says, eyeing Vanessa's picture with sympathy. The words resonate through me. *Only seventeen*. Vanessa is wearing a cardigan, though I know she'd hated it and argued vehemently against wearing it. Air. I need air. Outside. Need to get outside.

I stumble down the stairs, my breath coming out in short bursts. My thoughts separate and jumble into fragments that don't fit back together. The world continues to quake and blur like some strange painting. There are so many bodies, so many voices.

Then my fingertips brush the cool doorknob, and I pull it open. A girl complains at the cold. Quickly I step onto the front step and close the door behind me.

It's still raining out. The crowd on the porch is smaller, but not small enough. Pinpricks of wet seep into Lorna's dress and stick to my skin as I walk onto the lawn. Wind snatches at the skirt and goosebumps form. Forgot a coat again. Shuddering, I head for the cover of trees and darkness. I think of Amanda and her hidden cuts. Lorna and the bright blue of her computer screen. Mom and the *tap-tap-tap* of her keyboard. They have time to find their way.

And there's the truth I've been trying so hard to avoid, to smother, to hide.

I don't want to die.

I'm only seventeen.

All of it—Myers, the gloves, this haunting truth—is too much. Branches reach for my face as I run. Drenched leaves stick to my shoes. Not far enough, not far enough. But then I'm falling, and landing on my hands and knees. I don't get up. I sob there on the ground, hugging my middle. My hair trails through the mud. Thunder rumbles.

I can't remember the last time I cried, and now it's all I'm capable of. It consumes me. The tears, the ragged gulps, the explosion of salt on my tongue. My sobs echo through the trees.

Suddenly Myers is there.

"Ivy," he breathes, burying his fingers in my hair. Mindless of the storm, he brushes his lips over my cheeks, wiping the tears away. There's a tug, and suddenly my mask is gone. I blink up at him. Lightning flashes, and it seems as if he's glowing from the inside out, like some angel sent just for me. I shudder, and the sobs have stopped. I find it hard to remember why I'm even crying, why we're out here. None of it matters. All that matters is the way Myers trails his mouth over my closed eyes, how warm his palms are against my back.

Instinctively, I raise my face toward his, and he doesn't

hesitate. He devastates me with a real, tender, overwhelming kiss. I'm gripping his shoulders so tightly that it must be hurting him, as if he'll disappear or leave me in the darkness. But he doesn't. The taste of him is so familiar, yet so strange. It feels new and hot and painful. I know this won't—can't—happen again.

Myers leans over me, crushing me to the damp ground, and every lucid thought flaps away into the night. I gasp when he leaves a burning path of kisses down my neck and to my chest. I pull him back to me, wanting his lips back on mine. "I still love you," I hear myself whisper.

He doesn't say it back.

Cold air rushes into the space that's suddenly between us, and I blink up at Myers. His expression is twisted with anguish and fury. I'm so used to the reservation, the guarded smiles and the fathomless glint of emotion in his eyes, that I don't know what to say.

"I should go," he mutters thickly, turning away from me now.

"I know." A lump swells in my throat. Wet strands of hair clump in front of my eyes. I don't move to get up, not yet. There's still some part of me that hopes he'll come back. Even if every other part sees the moment is done, and so are we. Forever.

He pushes himself to his feet. Unable to face that expression again, I concentrate on the tips of his shoes again. "Good night, Ivy," he whispers. I want to beg him to stay, to choose me. I want to be selfish and pretend the numbers over my head aren't there.

I remain in the mud and rain, the night and trees, trying to find the will to get up and become Ivy again. The

Ivy that has no worries besides being the town leper or finishing Friday's assignment. Myers surprises me by pausing, though. "You look really beautiful," he adds, his expression just as sad as I feel.

I don't search for the right response, because there isn't one. And he's gone, anyway.

I close my eyes. Then I stand up, attempting in vain to straighten and fix the dress. The rain strengthens during the trek back to the house and my car. My mind is deliberately blank now. By the time I'm unlocking the door and putting the key in, I'm soaked. Lorna will be furious. The engine comes to life, and headlights shine over the field. The party shows no signs of tiring. Still, I head home.

Ten minutes later I park next to Mom's car and lose myself in the simplicity of the steps. Get out. Lock the car. Go up the stairs. Get inside. Shut the door. My shoes squeak on the floor, reminding me to stop and take them off. Spencer Hille singsongs a compliment, which I don't bother responding to. Bed. I just want to go to sleep. I'll figure out what to do about the gloves tomorrow.

I enter in a rush of rustles and repression. I don't turn on the lights. *You should get out of the dress*, reason says. Yet I find myself just moving to the bed.

I sink down onto the mattress—the springs groan—and my hand brushes something that doesn't belong. There's a piece of paper on the blanket. Frowning, I unfold it. In the dimness, my eyes scan the words. My heart stops. My lungs empty. My vision blurs. I read it again. And again.

The typed print is small and blocky.

Stop looking for me or you're next.

Chapter Fifteen

I've thought about how I'm going to die. Sometimes I imagine me and Uncle Nick in a car, suffering in a crash of metal. Other times I picture the diner on fire, being trapped and holding Uncle Nick's big hand as we inhale the smoke fumes and realize this is it.

But never did I think that Vanessa and I could meet the same fate.

It should be a good thing, really, that the killer is noticing me. It means I'm getting close. It could be a confirmation that Mitch Donovan really is the monster ruining all these lives. Maybe he was the one in the hallway, listening. Maybe he knows I found the gloves. I'm closer to all of this ending. It's good.

Yet as I sit on the front step, waiting for Allen to show up, all I can feel is fear. There's that sensation again, the one I had the night I found Vanessa in Havenger's Woods. Of time speeding up and slowing down at the same time.

The thought that keeps circling around and around in

my head is a distant, *He was in my room.* He walked past my mother and my sister. The floor moaned beneath his feet. He saw the four walls that protect me from the world each night, he touched the sheets I sleep in as he put down that piece of paper.

This changes everything.

I sit there, waiting some more, and the cold starts to get to me. The contacts in my eyes are stinging now. I huddle in my coat, my breath making white clouds in the air. My phone feels like a lump of ice in my hand. I stare down at it. Trace the numbers with my eyes. As if they have a mind of their own, my fingers reach out and touch *2*. Then I'm pressing it, listening to the phone.

They still haven't shut her cell off.

"Hi, you've got Vanessa. If I'm not answering, it's probably because I don't want to talk to you! But leave a message if you have to." Her voice is so melodic. The faint bite in her dulcet tones is easy to miss for those who didn't know her like I did. Closing my eyes, I hang up and call again. "Hi, you've got Vanessa..."

My gut twists. I shut the phone with a violent snap. The snow just keeps drifting gently, gently, oblivious to the violent storm inside of me. When did it start snowing?

Soon the headlights of Allen's car are swinging across the park, and his brakes squeal as he parks. Numbly, I hope that this visit doesn't wake Mom or Lorna. Allen heaves himself out of the seat. He's not in uniform. And he looks pissed.

"All right. What is this all about?" he grouses, approaching the step. I just hold the note out for him to take. He does. As he reads, his moustache twitches. "Where did you find this?" Allen finally asks. He surprises me by handing the paper back.

"In my room. On the bed." I take a breath. "Also, tonight I went to Mitch Donovan's Halloween party. I was in his room and found a pair of pink gloves. The same ones Jill Briggs had on the night she disappeared."

He processes my words. He doesn't say anything. After a few seconds, I frown. Why isn't he more excited about this?

Allen puts his hands on his hips, but the stance doesn't look so intimidating with his T-shirt flapping in the breeze. "What, exactly, are you expecting me to do?" he says after another long pause.

For a moment I just gape at him. Then I fly to my feet. "Are you kidding me? Go to the Donovans' and find the gloves! Maybe he saw me tonight, maybe this note is from *him*!" I shake the paper in Allen's face. "It's evidence that could help you! Look for prints or DNA—"

Allen scoffs. "This isn't one of those crime television shows, Ivy. It's Kennedy. My town, my department. And I won't be a laughingstock by claiming your little prank note there as 'evidence.'" He makes finger quotes in the air. "And you know as well as I do that Mitch Donovan has an alibi for Vanessa's case. Plus, I saw him myself during the time Jill Briggs vanished. He wouldn't have had time to go off and kidnap someone."

"Then why were the gloves—"

"You know, *you* were the last one to see Jill. And Vanessa, too. *You* were the only one who noticed these supposed gloves and found the body. Why is it *you're* always in the middle of these cases?"

I feel a muscle tic in my jaw. We glare at each other, me and this man who knows there's something different about Ivy Erickson. Something wrong. "It almost seems like you don't want to figure out who killed Vanessa," I remark, as if it's a statement about the gloom of the sky.

The sheriff's eyes narrow. "Careful, Ivy." He turns away, keys in hand.

"You're really not going to do anything?" I demand, disbelieving.

Allen opens his door, but takes the time to scowl at me. "You're lucky," he snaps. "I'm tempted to take you in right now. Pull me out of bed again, and next time I will." He gets back into the car.

No. I won't let him do this. Quickly, I stomp down the steps and run to the driver's window. I hit the glass, but Allen doesn't roll it down. I watch him switch gears. Forgetting about the sleeping world around us, I raise my voice over the engine and the wind. "It's not a goddamn prank—"

He drives away, leaving me in a cloud of exhaust. I clench my fists so hard it hurts. Fine. If he won't help me, I'll do this on my own.

Before I've finished the thought, it begins to snow.

• • •

Something has happened.

Whispers follow me to each class. I pick up only fragments, pieces. *He's crazy. How could he give it to her? She can't do it.* They glance at me out of the corner of their eyes and stop talking as soon as I'm near. After a few hours I can't take it anymore. At the end of fourth period I go in search of the one person at Kennedy High who will talk to me.

I find Amanda Ryan in the girls' bathroom; her familiar, worn shoes peek out from beneath one of the stalls. The air is rank with stale smoke. No one else is here, but that could change any second. Anxious and impatient, I rap on the door with the back of my knuckles. "Occupied," Amanda snaps. In my mind's eye I can see her swiftly dropping a cigarette in the toilet. Just a moment later the sound of its flush echoes off the walls.

"It's me," I say.

The door swings in, and her tall frame fills the space. She's smirking. "I hear congratulations are in order," Amanda replies, going to the sinks. I move to stand beside her, watching our reflections as she turns the faucet handle, then bends to cup the water and splash it on her face. Trying to get rid of the smell.

"Congratulations for what?"

Amanda keeps grinning. "Guess you'll see in about five minutes, won't you?" She brushes past me, and her scent is a combination of sweat and smoke.

I start to follow her. "Hey, wait—"

The door closes in my face. Gritting my teeth, I return to the mirror. *It doesn't bother you,* I tell myself. *None of it matters.*

Outside the auditorium there's a small gathering. I get closer, and Shannon turns her glare on me. Mitch glowers as if he's taken a bite of something sour. The sight of him causes a bad taste in my own mouth. Now isn't the time to wonder about what I found in his room, though. Frowning, I crane my neck to see what they're all looking at. Oddly enough, a few of them notice me and part to make room.

The weight of my classmates' attention is impossible to ignore. I hunch my shoulders against it as I go up to that piece of paper taped on the door. My eyes scan the words. I read it again.

This has to be some kind of mistake.

Turning my back on the list, I hurry into the auditorium. The lights are dimmed and the bright red of the chairs looks almost maroon in the darkness. Chuck is sitting in the front row, chewing on a pen and squinting down at the script. His large silhouette is unmistakable. Others have come in behind me, probably to see my reaction, but I hide behind my hair. I nearly trip in my haste down the center aisle. "Can I talk to you?" I blurt as soon as Chuck is within earshot.

He jumps, looking up at me with raised brows. He sees the way I fidget and a frown pulls down the corners of his mouth. "What is it?"

I glance at the class behind us. My teacher understands and gets up, his bones protesting. Together we ascend the stage stairs, walk across the platform, and reach the privacy of the wings. Chuck faces me, a tower of silence and expectation. I don't pause for breath or thought. "I can't be Emily," I whisper urgently. My eyes are wide with imploring, focused on the script he still holds. "I'm not an actress." I swallow hard.

Chuck doesn't speak for a moment. He appraises me. More panic makes its way up my throat, forms into words, but I don't let it out. The others will hear and judge. As always, I count the seconds. *One. Two. Three.* Finally, Chuck says, the words gentle, "You can do it, Ivy. I know you can. You proved that during the auditions."

I'm shaking my head before he's even finished. "If I had known that it was serious, I wouldn't have—"

"Wouldn't have tried?" he demands. He makes sure to keep his voice low. "I've been wrong to let you hide backstage. I should have known that you were capable of more than repairing costumes. Ivy, you need to let this town see you. Know that you're more."

"I'm not," I say instantly. "I'm not more. I'm exactly where I should be, and this part doesn't belong to me."

The teacher is looking at me with sorrow in his moss-green eyes. It would be so easy to tell him to go screw himself if he were wearing any other expression. "Yes, it does," he murmurs, like it's one of those obvious facts. The sky is blue. Kennedy is small. Before I can argue again, he lumbers back to his chair. "This isn't up for discussion. You auditioned, you got the part, and I expect to see you up on that stage every class period." The light shines down on him.

I stay where I am. It feels like I'm going to vomit. "Chuck, I can't—"

"Congratulations, Ivy." He leaves me in the darkness.

Yes, congratulations, Ivy, I hear Vanessa's voice hiss. I cringe, feeling the sharp sting of my nails digging into the soft flesh of my palms. This is her part. Everyone knows it. Once again the circumstances look so wrong, so twisted. Here I am stepping into my best friend's place, a hole I can't fill and a position in which I could never belong.

Just like the night I kissed her boyfriend.

Chapter Sixteen

It was during the summer. Mid-July. Vanessa was in the mood for a party, and when she put her mind to something, it usually happened. I did my best to talk her out of it; she didn't have any time left. Her numbers were nearly gone, and I selfishly wanted the final second to be just her and me, like it always had been. No peers to cause a panic, no doctors to prolong the inevitable. But she wouldn't listen to my objections, and eventually, I gave in. For Vanessa, a party seemed like the appropriate form of goodbye anyway. Poetic. Wasn't that the way everyone wanted to go?

Since Shannon Wyoming lives at the biggest place in town—not to mention her parents were visiting a sick grandmother that night—everyone gathered at her house. Vanessa rode with Brent. I went with Myers. I still remember the warmth of his hand on my knee, music drifting from the speakers in his truck. We didn't talk, really. That was the thing about Myers; he didn't speak unless he had something to say. I found his mere presence thrilling, comforting, enthralling. And that night, it was also the only thing keeping me sane. Instead of lamenting so much over a death I couldn't control, I focused on Myers. The moon shone through the driver's window, highlighting his profile. I leaned closer, pressing my smile into the curve between his shoulder and neck. I ran my finger down the slope of his nose. He pressed a feather-soft kiss to it when I reached his lips.

The truck went over a pothole, making my hip press into the square outline of his wallet, and I remembered. "Oh, did you find your credit card?"

Myers shook his head. "Called today and canceled it. I have a surprise for you. Later."

"What kind of surprise?"

He mock-glared. "The definition of a surprise is…well, I don't know the *Webster's* definition like you probably do, but I'm not going to reveal anything."

I was still smiling when he turned the truck into Shannon's driveway. That smile swiftly faded.

Every light in the house was on, sending square patterns over the wet lawn. There was nowhere to park, since every kid from school had come. Cars and pickups lined the length of the driveway. Myers stopped right where we were and put the gear into park. I leaned forward to see. Someone had brought alcohol, of course; one of the basketball players stood on the lawn, tipping his head back as he gulped down something in a red plastic cup. There was music playing. We could hear it even from inside the cab. It was loud enough to pound my thoughts back.

For a moment Myers and I just sat there. "Are you sure you want to go to this thing?" he asked.

"Vanessa wants me here."

I couldn't tell him that tonight was her last, and I *needed* to be there.

He didn't argue. Together, we got out. Myers held out his hand, and I took it gratefully. His palm was rough.

The air was warm and muggy. The rain had begun to let up; stray drops fell from the sky, quiet and serene. When we reached the steps Myers didn't bother knocking—there was no one around to hear it, anyway, I saw as the door swung inward. The house opened up into a living room, which was empty. Through the doorways, though, we could see kids in the dining room, the kitchen, and the living room. We plunged into the throng, and it felt as if I were leaving myself outside, where it was damp and real and Vanessa would always have some time left. Myers pulled me along. He was so solid.

Someone called Myers's name and he paused. "I see Vanessa," I said in his ear, hoping he wouldn't notice the way my voice broke. He didn't. My boyfriend simply kissed my cheek and I left his side.

"Where have you been?" Vanessa squealed when she spotted me. Before I could respond, she threw her arms around my body so enthusiastically it hurt. The scent of her shampoo surrounded me, too. Apples.

I managed to pull back a little, eyeing her. She wore a low-cut tank top and a pair of tight shorts. Her hair was long and slightly damp with sweat. This could easily have been from the heat and the dancing. "How much have you had to drink?" I asked, my glance involuntarily flicking up to her timer. Only four more hours. I stared at it longer than

I should have, trying to hide the way my eyes stung and my soul ached. "Did you remember to take your shots?"

Oblivious, my best friend pouted. "Ivy, come on. *Live* with me."

"I just don't want you to—"

"No, none of that! I won't listen to it tonight. Where's your drink? Guys, Ivy needs a drink!"

Like magic, someone handed Vanessa a cup, which she promptly shoved at me. Brown liquid sloshed and splashed over the rim. It was cold as it stained the front of my shirt. I sighed so she would think everything was normal, rolling my eyes, but Vanessa was determined.

"Drink," she ordered.

She wasn't going to give up until I did. Quickly I put the cup to my mouth and took a gulp that would satisfy her. I glared at her halfheartedly. "This is rum."

"It sure is. Take another sip."

I did, reluctantly. "Happy?"

"Not until you are, baby. Myers! Glad you could join us!" Vanessa waved with so much enthusiasm she almost stumbled. I steadied her. He gave her a bemused smile— the most she would get out of him. Vanessa focused on me again. "Come on, dance!" she pleaded.

"No one else is dancing," I protested.

"So what?"

She knew I couldn't refuse. There was just that magnetic force around Vanessa no one was able to resist. I still didn't know why she had chosen me to be the one she allowed inside. So I let her spin us, succumbed to her urges and drank from the red cup some more. I'd always been a lightweight; already I could feel the effects of it.

For an hour we danced and laughed. I committed her face to memory, cherished her warmth, adored her freedom. Colors blended together and the music became a meaningless hum. Eventually Vanessa dragged Brent into the center of the room, and he shuffled his feet uncomfortably. I pressed my back to a wall, breathing hard. Somehow the cup was still in my hand. As I watched my classmates, I took another drink.

All of the numbers were crowded together until the glow was almost blinding, like a blanket of clouds readying for a storm. So much time. So little time. None of them knew. They were beautifully oblivious as they danced closer and closer to their endings. There was Gregory Yang, who would die at thirty-two years old, probably from his drug habits, if I had to guess. And Emma Baker, the freshman who dreamed of being a concert pianist, would leave this world at twenty-four.

Vanessa still had three hours left.

Mitch was trying to intervene now. The doting brother who would live far beyond his sister for sixty-one years. His expression was tight and worried as he fought his way through the crowd. He reached for her arm in an attempt to pull her away. Vanessa, of course, evaded his grasp and laughed. He said something that made her smile transform to a scowl.

As I watched her, whatever semblance of acceptance I'd managed to find faded. I couldn't let her go. Not without trying to stop it. She wasn't going to die from diabetes; I would *make* her take those shots. I started toward Vanessa, but paused when she cuddled into Brent's chest, looking so utterly happy that it seemed impossible that anything could change it.

An hour. I'd give her one more hour to enjoy this party.

Dizzy, I went to find Myers. Not in the living room. Not in the kitchen. I trailed my fingers along the striped wallpaper in the dining room and saw him in the corner. He was talking to Tommy, the point guard. He nodded. I stood there for a moment, looking at their numbers, too. Myers was different from everyone else. Somehow, he'd made me forget. He didn't deserve to love and to lose. He deserved forever.

Forever was an impossibility with me.

I stumbled away. I began to search for somewhere I could escape the noise, the timers. In the hallway, my fingers collided with a doorknob. Pushing aside the couple making out in front of it—the girl, Nicole, called me a bitch, and unfortunately she wouldn't bite it for another forty-nine years—I ducked inside. I didn't even care what it was. A closet, a bathroom. But as I backed up, my heel dangled over nothingness. Cautiously, I reached down with my foot. Stairs. This must lead to the basement. I used the walls on either side for support and managed not to trip. At the bottom there was thick carpet. I took off my shoes, not wanting to leave stains even in my drunken state. I bumped into something soft and plush, level with my thighs. A couch. There in the dark I sank down, trying not to capitulate to the despair that so often lurked within my own heart.

Without the numbers everywhere and no mirrors hanging up, it was easy to lose track of the seconds and forget about my best friend. The music changed three times. To distract myself, I sang in a shaking whisper. A lullaby Mom used to croon before Dad left. But the rum made it hard to recall the exact words. Something about hummingbirds and spring...

"Hiding again?"

I jumped. *Hiccup.* "W-who's there?"

Light flooded the den. Blinking, I relaxed when I saw that it was just Brent standing at the end of the couch. Sweat gleamed on his forehead, and he looked just as weary as I felt. Vanessa did that to people. Made them believe they were the center of her universe, made them give her everything, and then she spun away until all that was left was her memory. I smiled at him, swaying. *Hiccup.* He had no idea that the center of our universe was about to spin away permanently.

No, I would stop it.

Brent raised his brows, and I remembered that he'd asked a question. "Just taking a break," I mumbled.

He sat down. The cushions deflated from the added weight, causing me to slide toward him. I caught myself, giggling. "A break from what?" Brent asked now, grinning.

Just like that, I sobered. Flashes hit me, images. The hours hovering over my best friend. The shrinking days above my own head. It was easy to picture the gravestones and the people we'd leave behind.

Trying to hide my thoughts, I made a vague gesture toward the stairs. "All of it," I said to Brent. Was I slurring?

He knew something was wrong. "So, hiding."

I managed a faint smile. "Yeah, I guess so." A distant part of my mind urged me to get back to Vanessa, but I didn't move.

We fell silent. Oddly enough, it wasn't uncomfortable. The party raged in the rest of the house, and I remained in my bubble of solidarity with Brent Nordstrom. Now that the light was on, I could study our surroundings. A giant flat-screen took up the wall in front of us, and the others had been decorated with animal heads. The eyes of frozen deer and fish looked at me and knew my secrets. Suddenly it didn't feel so much like a haven. Paranoia edged in.

"I just realized. I've known you my entire life, but I don't *know* you at all," Brent ventured, distracting me. His voice, though normal, felt like a scream in the stillness.

Once they registered, the words surprised me. "There's not much to know," I mumbled, bringing my knees to my chest. Protecting myself from his friendliness, his curiosity. I glanced at the stairs. Myers and Vanessa would be looking for me. She was so close to zero. I knew that, even if the rum didn't want me to. Why, then, didn't it feel so important at that moment?

Five minutes, I decided. I'd go upstairs in five minutes.

Brent ignored my obvious discomfort. "I doubt that."

I turned my head to meet his gaze. He was looking at me strangely. Differently. Suddenly my throat was too dry, and I swallowed. "Why are you down here?" I asked, in an attempt to steer the conversation to safer places.

Thankfully, he didn't push it. Instead, he sat back, sighing. "Vanessa can be a little overwhelming sometimes. Well, you know. I needed a second away from all the cheerleader talk and prom plans."

I frowned. "I thought you liked that kind of stuff."

He uttered a sound that was supposed to be a laugh,

but didn't quite succeed. "I like *Vanessa*. Sometimes I think she forgets I'm a guy."

"That's pretty much impossible." I said it without thinking. Then I realized that I'd uttered the thought out loud, and heat spread through my cheeks. I didn't dare look at Brent again, but I knew he was still watching me in a strange, fathomless way that made my stomach flutter. I swallowed. "I never got to tell you how great you played in that last football game, by the way. I know it was a while ago, but that last play was amazing."

He shifted, and it brought him closer. I didn't move. "You were there?"

I lost myself in the patterns of the rug. "In the bleachers. Where I always am."

"You shouldn't hide so much," he said, tucking a stray curl behind my ear. It was so startling that I let out a small gasp. Though my instincts urged me to bolt up from the couch, something else kept me there. My veins were singing, and something deep inside wanted to be impulsive again, despite my vows of reformation. To seize anything and everything while I could. Was it that damn rum? Or just my hatred of the numbers, a flame that constantly simmered at my core? "I should…I should go find…" I stuttered.

He breathed my name as if it were a drug: "*Ivy*."

Brent leaned toward me as if he'd always wanted to do it. I could have stopped him, I could have said no. But I didn't. It was my choice. Maybe I let it happen because I didn't want to die having only kissed one boy. Maybe it was just habit, doing something forbidden and reckless. Or maybe I just wanted everyone to hate me. Whatever the reason, Brent's lips brushed mine. He smelled of cologne and beer and sweat. I put my hand on his chest, which Brent took as an invitation. He shoved his tongue in my mouth, forcing it open. He tasted awful.

As quickly as it had begun, I wanted it over. Guilt shattered through the numbed barrier the alcohol had put up. What was I doing? I had a boyfriend, he had a girlfriend. *Vanessa.* My best friend. *Myers.* The love of my life. Brent and I couldn't do this. It would ruin everything. Tears sprang to my eyes as I remembered all of the wonderful moments with Myers. Quiet evenings in his truck and passionate nights in his room. Mist spreading across the lake and steam clouding the curtained windows. Then I thought of all those afternoons with Vanessa, doing homework and talking about the most secret of things. Curtains fluttering in the breeze.

Vanessa and I would never have another afternoon like that again.

I needed to find her *now*.

"Brent, no. Stop." It came out as a whisper. He didn't hear me. He was kissing the tender skin of my stomach—somehow he'd unbuttoned my shirt without my realizing it—and anguish crashed over me like a concrete wave. All I could see now was their faces, and I knew this couldn't happen. "Brent, please—"

"Ivy?"

Brent and I sprang apart. He actually fell to the floor, a mess of elbows and knees. I gasped, grasping for the buttons on my shirt. But it was too late. Too late.

Myers stood in the doorway.

Chapter Seventeen

I wake up on my feet.

Cold. Dark. Glittering snow. I shiver, huddling into myself, and stare at Vanessa's window. It's happened later than usual this time. All around, the night is utterly black, no hint of dawn to be seen. Even Idiot is silent. I glance up at the sky and note that no stars are out.

The silence is overwhelming. For the first time, I don't stand under the streetlight, lingering in the cruel wind. I go to that window.

Once I'm standing next to the trailer, though, I realize it's too dark inside to see anything. Suddenly I'm reaching out to open it. Unsurprisingly, the window isn't locked. Kennedy used to be a place where nothing bad happened, and old habits die hard. I lift the frame and climb inside with no difficulty.

It smells musty. I look around, breathing hard and fast. I almost say her name. The room is empty, of course... but not to me. I don't need to close my eyes to see where her bed once was, where the vanity stood, all the colorful clothes hanging in her closet, all the smiling pictures covering her walls.

I can't stop myself from going back, remembering.

The sheet glows around us, lit like a lantern with the flame in its center. "There," Vanessa announces, forgetting to keep her voice low. She sits back with a triumphant smile. I look at the sign she's made for our fortress. The letters are crooked, vibrant strokes of marker. THIS IS THE CASTLE OF VANESSA AND IVY. ENTER AT YOUR PERIL. The tape is already coming off the sheet, but I won't tell her.

"No one else can come in but me?" I ask her, hugging my knees. The frogs on my pajama pants grin up at us.

My best friend shakes her bright head. "Nope. Especially not Mitch! He'll try to, you know. He always tries." She settles onto her sleeping bag and fusses with a doll. I watch her, wishing I were as brave and pretty as her. But it's okay I'm not. It's enough that, for some reason, she picked me to be the one she trusted.

Soon Vanessa's eyelids droop. She lies down. Her breath smells like bubblegum toothpaste. "Promise that we'll be friends forever," she whispers, pressing her forehead to mine.

"I promise," I whisper back.

She lets out a sigh, as if a great weight has been lifted from her shoulders. Her eyelashes flutter and go completely still. But I don't follow her into the dream, not yet. For a moment I make shadows on the illuminated side of the sheet. A bird, a dog. I giggle.

Vanessa frowns sleepily. "Go to sleep, Ivy. We're safe in the castle." She wraps her little arm around me.

"'Night, Nessa," I say, absorbing her warmth. Then I close my eyes, too, and the castle guards us as we slumber.

There's a lump in my throat. Moving away from the center of the room, I touch one of the walls. This was where her desk was. I look down and see it, a ghostly image. I still remember the note I found the night she was killed, when I'd rushed into her room and found it empty. I'd been ready—no, *determined* to make her listen to another apology for what happened at the party earlier. To break all my own rules and try saving her, despite the futility of it. The note rested there, a single piece of paper. In type it read, *Meet me in Havenger's Woods.* The killer must have gone back to the trailer after killing Vanessa and taken it, because when Allen and his men searched her room, it was nowhere to be found.

Wait.

I frown. There'd been something else by the note. A flower beside it, a splash of white. Until now I'd never given it much thought. There'd only been the importance of those printed words.

A gardenia.

I picture it lying there, the darkening petals against the wood of the desk. I'd been in too much of a hurry to care. Maybe I'd subconsciously assumed it was from Brent. My heart pounds harder. Why was it there? Vanessa hated flowers. She said if anyone was going to give her something, it should be jewelry or candy, something she could keep or enjoy. Flowers only wilted and died. She couldn't have changed so much in those last months. The gardenia was wrong. A mark, an omen.

A clue.

Chapter Eighteen

The world I know has been hidden beneath a layer of clean, fresh snow. Icicles dangle from the roof of Hallett Cottages, and already the sunlight is melting them. Water drips down and puddles on the window sill. I touch the glass. My skin cools instantly as winter reaches back. It can't get to me, though. Not in here.

"Are you all right, Hannah? You're quiet today."

Turning, I manage a smile at Miranda. She hasn't remembered who I am for a few days now, and pretending to be her daughter has become second nature. "I'm fine. Just tired."

She's sitting on her bed, the model example of prim posture and pressed clothing. Today she's wearing a blue blouse with gray slacks that look like they're from the seventies. And they probably are. Her hair is permed to perfection. "You shouldn't work so hard," she chides. "I know you want to go to college, honey, but you don't need *all* those extracurriculars on your résumé."

"I'm not going to college." It just pops out. They're Ivy's words, not Hannah's.

Miranda blinks. "What are you going to do, then?" she asks. There's no chance to answer; her expression brightens. "Did David propose?" There's a note of true excitement in her voice. Suddenly she's the most animated I've ever seen her. The realization hits me: it's the prospect of her dead daughter moving on, becoming more. That's what Miranda Raspberry wants most in the world. Her final wish. This is what I've been looking for.

And for the first time, I can't bring myself to lie to her. Not even knowing that she has sixteen days left makes telling the pretty stories any easier. Not this time. Maybe it's because I've been thinking of my own days so much, and I realized that I would want the ugly truths over all of the beautiful lies. I hesitate, and Miranda beams expectantly. In these parts, kids have a tendency to marry young. "No, I'm not getting married, either, Mom," I say, biting my lip.

Her disappointment is so strong that she actually sets her needlepoint down. "Then what are you going to do, Hannah?" she asks anxiously. Her forehead wrinkles.

Hating that I've caused her worry, I turn my face back toward the window. The white light of morning cascades over my skin. Vanessa whispers in my head. She's been getting louder and louder. *Live with me, Ivy.*

I give the old, dying woman something that is part lie, part truth, as most things are.

"I'm going to live."

• • •

After our first play rehearsal—we all sat in chairs that formed a circle and read from Chuck's script—I visit Russell. He tells another story about his son, but it's difficult to listen. There's a part of me that wants to go back to the Donovan house, go through Mitch's room again and find something more concrete to give Allen. But there's too much risk, especially now that I'm getting threatening notes. I need to figure out another way to get the truth, like using the gardenia.

Next I go straight to the diner. My veins are humming, and my break can't come soon enough. I want to investigate that flower. Tonight Amar's singing grates on my nerves and I can't bring myself to laugh at Susie's dirty jokes. It isn't very busy, thankfully, so I slip out of the kitchen the first chance I get. Uncle Nick doesn't notice me passing his office as I open the back door. It shuts behind me with a gentle *click*.

The night air is particularly frigid, and it snatches greedily at the warmth of my breath. There's a single light over the doorway. Out here, there's nothing but the dumpsters and the trees to hear what I'm about to do. Pulling out the list of names I'd made during lunch, along with my phone, I sit down on the cement step and type the first number into the keypad. I wrap my other arm around my torso, realizing that I forgot to grab a coat. Again.

It rings twice before a female voice greets me. My stomach flutters. "Hi, Wendy," I say, trying to sound normal. "This is Ivy Erickson."

"Ivy, hi!" she chirps. "This is a first. Who do you want to send flowers to?"

"No, I'm not calling about sending flowers. I'm sorry. This might sound strange, but I'm wondering if anyone around here ordered gardenias in the past few months. Maybe around July?"

Wendy hesitates. She probably decides not to ask any questions. "Well, I do keep receipts. Your uncle convinced me to do it. Apparently it's important to keep records. Anyway, hold on." There's a *thud*, and then nothing. My knee jiggles up and down. The trees watch and wait with me. Exactly nine seconds later Wendy's voice sounds in my ear again. "Can you believe it's already November?" she asks. "It's crazy how quickly times goes by. Now what was the month again? Ah, yes. July…July…no, looks like I didn't sell any gardenias. Not before or after that either, as far as I can tell. What's this all about?"

I release a breath. "Nothing. Never mind."

I press the end button and glance at the next shop on the list. It's for the only florist in Stephen, a small town about fifteen minutes south of here. This time it rings three times and I find myself talking to a male employee. He's initially reluctant to give me what I want, but I convince him with a lie about receiving a bouquet and wanting to find out who my secret admirer is. Nothing for gardenias in the months surrounding July. Same with the florist in Warren, it turns out when I keep going. It's even farther south, about forty minutes. Or Hallock, which is just a few minutes north. Next I try Donaldson, a town that is also nearby. When I'm again met with disappointment, an odd frenzy creeps over me. Shivering, I disregard my shift entirely and call every single florist on the list. Halma, Humboldt, Lake Bronson, Lancaster, Saint Vincent.

All dead ends or no answers.

Finally I call the Karlstad florists—it's the biggest town

around, a half hour east of Kennedy—and there's no answer for any of them. I leave short messages with just my name and number. Then I just sit there for a few seconds, staring at the faint glow of the moon, hidden behind clouds. My break is *definitely* over, but I still don't get up.

"Hey, Ivy."

I cry out, scrambling to my feet. Brent Nordstrom stands in front of the door, hands shoved in his pockets. For a moment I can't speak as relief overwhelms me. Brent. Just Brent. Not someone else, who leaves notes and pretty flowers for young girls. I stare at him and realize that I haven't really *looked* at him in such a long time. His hair is longer than he used to wear it, tousled. It makes him look like a little boy. He's wearing a bright yellow jersey that he's had since middle school. "What the hell are you doing out here?" I finally snap, trying to calm my racing heart. How did he know I was back here? *He must have been watching you*, a voice whispers. I clench my fists.

"Looking for you," Brent answers quietly. There's that subtle note of beseeching in his voice.

"Well, you found me. Now leave me alone."

Brent doesn't move, which is new. He's always given up before. "I'm just trying to warn you, Ivy," he says. He's nervous; his glance darts around as if someone might be hiding in the dumpster. He rubs the back of his neck, and I see a bandage on his hand. I don't care enough to ask him how he got it.

I want him gone. I want my memories of him somewhere else where they can't affect me. But I can't help thinking of my numbers and the note on my bed, and I know I need to listen. "Warn me about what?" I ask, wary.

Resentful. I wish I could blame him entirely for that night, but I can't. Not when I stayed on that couch and let him kiss me.

Mindless of my internal struggle, Brent takes another step, drawing closer to me. He says the words so that only I will hear. "Mitch is getting worse. His parents are being hard on him for the Halloween party, and he's in lockdown. I think the quiet is getting to him, and he's been talking about you. A lot." His Adam's apple bobs. He's actually frightened.

Mitch's accusation comes back. I remember the wildness in his eyes. *You betrayed her. She was your best friend.* Trying to hide the way my insides quake, I raise my gaze and meet Brent's earnest one. "What is he saying?"

He falters. His timer makes the hesitation all the more obvious as it marks the seconds. "You just need to be careful, all right? Don't go anywhere alone."

If anything, my resentment toward him increases because he's given me more to fear. It's a metallic taste in my mouth. "Fine," I say through my teeth. When he doesn't leave, I glare. "Is there something else? Another cryptic warning? More helpful, super-specific advice?"

"*I'm sorry, Ivy,*" he snaps right back. The force of his tone startles me into silence. "It was wrong to kiss you that night," he goes on, taking advantage of the moment. "Even though it happened months ago, I need to say it. I've picked up the phone to call you a hundred times. I've tried to say something in school. I know you hate me, and I deserve it. Every bit of it. But I miss her too, goddamn it. I loved her too. So stop acting like you're the only one that lost her."

All this time, I thought the two of us had an unspoken agreement to never acknowledge what happened that night. Now that he's broken it, I don't know how to react. Somewhere an engine starts, and the sound vibrates through the night—it barely penetrates my churning thoughts. Brent has no idea that because of what we did, because of Vanessa's resulting hatred, she died alone.

I realize I'm smiling. But it's a bitter, angry smile. "You don't know anything, Brent."

Allen's stepson doesn't relent. There's an expression in his eyes I can't discern. Hurt, maybe? "I probably don't. But *at least I'm trying to move on.*" He waits for me to respond, and when I don't, he finally turns his back on me. The door slams. I stand there, trying to stay afloat in a wave of feeling.

The sound of my phone ringing shatters the stillness. Without thinking about it, I hit TALK and hold the speaker to my ear. "Hello?"

"Is this Ivy?" A relaxed drawl. A woman.

"Yes."

"This is Martha Reynolds, with Roses and Bouquets? You left a message to contact you as soon as possible?"

It takes me a moment. But then I remember the list of florists in my pocket and the gardenia. The encounter with Brent fades as I hurry to say, "Oh! Yeah, thank you so much for calling me back." I swallow. "It's kind of a strange request, but I was wondering if you had any purchases for gardenias around July of this year. I know that was a while ago, but if you still have a name—"

"I can't just give out that information, honey."

"Please. This is important. You have no idea how important."

There's the sound of papers rustling. "All right," Martha sighs. "Yes, I did have a few gardenia sales. The first customer paid with cash, so I can't help you with that one. The second one was for a Keith Barns. The third one…his signature is really hard to make out. But it looks like the last one was purchased by…"

Once again my pulse thumps harder and faster. *Tell me the name!* I want to scream. Instead I reply, the word strangled, "Yes?"

"Miles? Marcus? No, wait." Then she says it.

Everything inside me freezes. Thoughts, blood, heartbeat. "I'm sorry. Could you repeat that?"

"Myers Patripski. The name is Myers Patripski."

Chapter Nineteen

There's a knock at the door.

I lie in bed curled under a pile of blankets, since the thermostat is still too low. I don't react to the sound. Mom knocks again and her voice drifts through a second later. "Ivy? Are you in there?"

"Yes."

At this, Mom finally pokes her head in. Just so that I can see only a portion of her eyes and nose. It's disorienting from this angle, as if I'm looking at a Picasso painting. "You didn't wake me up this morning," she says. Her nametag glints—at least she's dressed. The clock next to me reads 8:03. "Is everything okay?"

It's too bright outside. I close my eyes. "I don't feel good," I mumble after a silence that's too long. "I think I'll stay home today."

Mom doesn't argue. All she says is, "All right." She probably doesn't know how to tell me no; she's never been that kind of mother. Sometimes I hate her for it. Sometimes

I wish she were the kind of mother to make me lunches, to go school shopping, to ask about friends and boys and sex. Now she just studies me, remaining behind that crack in the door as if she's afraid to come in. "Well, Lorna is here, if you need anything," she tells me.

"I know."

"Hey, did you hear about that other girl?"

This gains my attention. I lift my head, just a little, and frown. "What girl?"

Her lips press into a thin line. "The police found a girl's body. In Crookston, I guess. At breakfast one of the deputies let it slip that this girl might have managed to bite whoever did it. Something about blood in her teeth." She says more that I don't hear and waits for a response, but I've sunk back into the mattress. Now all I can think is, *Another one. Was it Mitch? Was it Myers? Not another one.*

The hinges squeal as Mom backs away. "I'll see you tonight, then. Don't worry about your shift. I'll talk to Nick."

"Thanks," I say bleakly.

"You're welcome. Feel better."

She closes the door.

• • •

It snows.

Idiot sniffs my limp hands. After a moment he nudges them with his big head, wanting to be touched. Wanting to be loved. His whiskers tickle. I just sit there on the front step of the trailer, huddling in my coat and staring out at the dull sunset. A snowflake lands on my arm, and I look down at it for a moment. The icy design is intricate against the solid color of my sleeve.

I keep going over the conversation with Martha again and again in my head. Idiot loses interest and wanders away.

That can't be right. Did you see the person who signed the name? Do you remember what he looked like?

Honey, I can't remember last week.

Please think. Please.

Okay, okay. Hold on. Let's see. Myers Patripski. Myers Patripski. July…gardenia…Wait. Damn! I think I do remember. It was a kid. A boy. Yeah, I thought it was strange that someone so young was buying such a big order. Of gardenias, no less. But his card went through without a problem.

What do you mean, "such a big order"?

The kid bought three giant bouquets. Enough to start his own crop, if he wanted to.

Another memory keeps taunting me, one from this summer—Myers saying his credit card was stolen. He could have been lying, and it took him a long time to supposedly cancel it. But why would he mention it at all if he did use his card to buy the gardenias? I hadn't seen the flower at that point. It doesn't make any sense.

The door opens, and a triangle of light floods the steps. The thin layer of snow over the walkway glitters. "Ivy, come inside!" Mom snaps. Her silhouette lengthens and shivers. "You're going to catch pneumonia!"

"Okay, Mom."

As she retreats I hear her muttering, "That could be an interesting way to die…"

Warmth caresses my back, a beckon to go inside, to

lose myself in dreams. But I can't. I close my eyes and think of Myers, the boy I will always love. His brown eyes, his stubborn curls, that dimple in his left cheek, the rough skin of his palms.

A killer.

In the cold I become a metronome, ticking back and forth between the choices. Confront. Avoid. Demand. Pretend.

I have to know.

I surge to my feet and leave a trail of footprints going to my car. The door groans as I get in, and a moment later my headlights illuminate the park. Mom must have been coming back out to check on me, because her voice slices through the stillness. "Ivy, where are you—"

I'm already gone.

Chapter Twenty

It feels as if the house has been waiting for me.

Twilight has come and gone. The only light to guide my way up the sidewalk shines through an upstairs window. I know whose room that is, even with the curtains drawn. My pulse quickens from both fear and anticipation. Myers. So many hours we spent in that room, entwined, talking about everything and nothing. I fiddle with my keys all the way to the door.

It's late. I didn't really think about inconsequential things like who might be sleeping when I set out to find the truth. Now I remember Myers's sisters, his dad. *Too late to go back now.* I raise my hand and knock. Silence. I shift from foot to foot, mutely telling my pulse to quiet, calm, be still. I can do this. I *need* to do this.

Then why do I want to run so badly?

Eighteen seconds go by. My fist is poised to knock again when I hear it. Footsteps. Slow. Tired. Suddenly the porch light flicks on with an audible sound, and electricity hums. I stop breathing.

The door opens, and there he is. Wearing nothing but a pair of boxer shorts, with heavy-lidded eyes and an expression that's just a little annoyed. His hair is a tousled mess. When Myers sees it's me, though, those eyes widen. "Ivy?" His voice is scratchy. He says it as if I'm an apparition, as if he doesn't believe it.

I don't bother with pretense or politeness. "I need to ask you something."

Myers glances behind him, then opens the door wider. "Come in. It's freezing out there."

After an instant of hesitation, I step over the threshold. The smell in here is so familiar it causes a twinge in my chest. Like pinecones and spaghetti. No one in the Patripski family knows how to cook, so it's usually the same meals every week. I brush past Myers, careful not to let my gaze linger on his bare chest. My stomach is wild with wings and air.

"Not here," Myers mutters. He doesn't look, but I do. The door to the basement is open. Voices float up the stairs, probably the television. His dad is home.

"Your room?" I ask. Myers nods. My feet need no prompting; they remember the way. Up the stairs, down the narrow hall, last door on the left. Myers maintains a safe distance between us. His bedroom door is open, but I pause in front of it.

"Go ahead," he says. Still tentative, I take four steps and stop in the middle of his space. Myers shuts the door behind him and moves past.

The scents in here do things to me. Cologne, detergent,

Myers. I can't stop myself from looking around, remembering. A lump forms in my throat. It hasn't changed. Not the green walls, the rumpled covers of his bed, the clothes abandoned everywhere other than in the laundry basket. And on his nightstand—breath catches in my throat when I see that he still has the framed picture of us there.

Trying to hide how it affects me, I face Myers but concentrate on the wood floor. I concentrate on the wood floor. There are three seconds of uncomfortable, searing silence. Then, somehow, I make myself look up and say it. "I know about you going to Karlstad. I know why."

Myers freezes just as he's reaching for a rumpled T-shirt by the bed. He straightens, staring at me. His jaw works. His expression is unfathomable. "How did you find out?" he asks finally.

In that moment, I realize that I wanted him to deny it. To tell me that I'm wrong, I'm crazy, it's impossible. "I made some calls," I reply faintly. I think I can hear my heart breaking.

Now Myers frowns. "Who the hell did you call? The only people I told were a couple buddies at the yard."

"What?" I shake my head. "Wait, told them what?"

Quickly, he yanks the shirt over his head. I hate how I watch his muscles move. "I'm talking about the jeweler," he snaps. "What are *you* talking about?" The picture catches his attention and in two quick strides he goes to the nightstand, picks it up, and shoves it in a drawer.

I won't let him confuse me. "I'm talking about the *florist*. The gardenias. Vanessa, Jill, the others." I swallow. "I know everything, Myers."

My ex-boyfriend shakes his head, looking sincerely baffled. "I have no idea what you're talking about."

"If you didn't go to Roses and Bouquets, then why were you in Karlstad?" I challenge, sick of all the lies, the facades.

Even after I've uttered the name of the shop out loud, Myers still looks bewildered. But this question makes him hesitate. "I wanted it to be a surprise." He sits down on the bed. The mattress squeaks.

It seems as if he expects me to make a connection, but I don't understand. "What surprise?" I ask. It comes out quiet, uncertain. There's a tight sensation in my chest. Am I wrong about Myers?

He rubs the back of his neck. There's a pained look in his eyes. Finally he says, the words a resigned sigh, "I bought you a ring. I was going to propose the night of Vanessa's party."

Chapter Twenty-One

I stare at him.

He can't meet my eyes, though. The numbers above him glow brighter, it seems, as they mark how long the quiet lingers. Ten seconds. Fifteen. Twenty. On the twenty-third second I clear my throat. "You…" I start. Stop. Begin again. "You were going to…"

Myers makes another helpless gesture. "I had it planned out. On the way home I was going to pull over and get some picnic stuff out of the back. The ring was in my pocket," he adds wearily. "But then everything happened. You and Brent. Vanessa."

He says something else, but I don't hear it. There's a pain in my chest. The walls are closing in. "That's all in the past now, I guess," I say, forcing a smile. It's the hardest thing I've ever done. Maybe it's selfish, but I wish his excuse for being in Karlstad was anything else. Anything but this, the future I've lost.

As if he feels the same regret I do—which he can't,

because that would mean he still loves me just as much as I love him—Myers closes his eyes. His fingers lace in front of him, between his knees, like he's restraining himself. Those hands will never touch me again, no matter how much I want them to. I feel sick.

"Ivy, you know that's not true," Myers whispers.

It needs to be. I shake my head again. I'm backing away, almost involuntarily. Maybe part of me secretly thought we would find a way to be together. Until the end. This revelation is a shattering reminder that I'm only fooling myself, trying to repair what should stay broken. "It is, actually. So it's good that you have Ginger now. It's good that you have Ginger now." My back bumps into the wall. I reach behind me, fumbling for the doorknob.

Myers stands so abruptly that I jump. "I'm not with Ginger," he says. "I mean, I was. For one night. But that's it. I told you we were together because I wanted to hurt you."

It takes a moment for me to understand. In the meantime, Myers notices the distance I'm putting between us. "Don't," he growls. And he moves across the room to stand in front of me, making it impossible to open the door.

I'm frozen now. Stuck in place by some nameless desire, sparked by his expression. "Don't what?" It comes out as a glass whisper. Transparent, entirely breakable.

His breath tickles my bottom lip. "Don't do this. Not with me," he whispers back. Heat coils in my belly. *No more talking*, I nearly say.

Suddenly I hate him. It feels like he's betrayed me, even though I'm the one that ruined us. I try not to imagine him touching *her*, but I can't stop it. Bile rises in my throat. "Is this payback?" I spit. "You wanted me to feel what you felt, all those months ago?" I shove him.

Myers stumbles. "You want the truth?" he asks, recovering. "I slept with Ginger one time, just once, and that was only because I'd already tried everything else to forget you. I almost threw up." He clenches his fists. His words sink in, and I don't know what to say. I can't say anything.

It turns out I don't need to; he isn't finished. "I avoided her for days afterward," Myers goes on, anguished. He's moving away from me now. "Then one day she came to the yard and told me how she felt. Even though I told her I didn't—couldn't—feel the same way, she won't let go. That's what we were arguing about on the afternoon you gave me a ride." He sits down on his bed again, cradling his head. "Do you have any idea how much I hate this, Ivy? I've never been the kind of guy to do that to someone."

Slowly, timidly, I approach and settle beside him. He doesn't react. I dare to touch his shoulder. His skin is warm through the thin material of the shirt. Somehow I know the real source of his torment, in this moment. "You're not your dad, Myers. You never could be," I murmur.

He laughs, a mirthless sound. "Sure doesn't feel that way."

"People make mistakes," I remind him quietly. "I know that better than anyone, right? Sometimes those mistakes feel so big and awful that it's easy to believe we'll never recover from them. Yet somehow, we do."

Shocking me, Myers reaches up and tangles his fingers with mine. He releases a ragged breath and doesn't say anything else. We sit like that for seventeen seconds. It feels as if my hand is disconnected from my body, as if it's the only part of me that's real. But no matter how much I want to, I can't forget about time. I don't belong here anymore. Maybe I never did. "I should go," I say, pulling myself free.

At this, Myers turns. Our eyes meet. "We should do a lot of things." He brushes a curl out of my face.

Just that single touch of his fingers makes my resolve buckle. Does this mean he forgives me? No, no, he needs to hate me. "We shouldn't..."

His voice is more level than mine. "Why not?"

Should. Shouldn't. Suddenly it doesn't matter. Time ceases to exist, and I forget each and every one of my reasons for stopping it. He leans close enough that I can feel his words on my cheek. "Do you know how good you smell?" he whispers. "I've missed that. Every day." He hesitates.

Trying not to reveal my desperation, my eagerness, my *need*, I don't speak. Myers moans. "Why is it impossible to stay mad at you, Ivy?" Slowly, his lips graze the edge of my jaw, skim my temple. I bury my fingers in his covers to restrain myself. What if he changes his mind?

Then Myers kisses the curve between my neck and shoulder. It has all the effect of fire. I burn.

Just like that, it's easy to disregard all the vulnerability and doubt. Turning, I rest my hand on his chest, right in the center so my thumb rests on the hollow of his throat. Something in me expands and soars at the feel of his pulse: hard and racing, as if he's just run for miles. "Myers," I breathe, loving it, loving him.

As soon as I utter his name, the space between us vanishes. Myers leans in, kissing me hard. Once. Twice. Slowly, I tilt back. He lowers himself onto me, a welcome weight that makes other places on my body ignite. He opens his mouth, and my own lips part. Our tongues touch, and the taste of him is electric. I gasp, and this seems to drive him mad. Our breathing quickens and the air is hot, so hot. He runs his rough palm up my bare stomach, and I push myself into him even though there's absolutely nothing between us.

The blood surging through my veins is pulsing. It's impossible to form a coherent thought. My entire world is Myers. I close my eyes, darkness upon darkness, and drown in the shivering sensation of his nearness. No walls, no restraint. He smells like winter and the musky hint of boy.

And in that moment between floating and soaring, I whisper, "I would have said yes." The words are so quiet I'm not sure if he hears them, but then his arms tighten, and I know he has.

For the first time in months, for the hundredth time in his arms, I forget about the numbers.

· · ·

I leave while he's sleeping.

The house watches me slip into the hallway, creak down the stairs, and slip out the front door. The cold sinks eagerly into my bones as soon as I step onto the porch and my ragged breath swirls through the air. My glasses go cloudy. On the sidewalk I glance up at that window. It looks unreal through the frost, as if it isn't part of this world. I close my eyes and imagine the sleeping boy there, remember how it felt to kiss his soft lips, how dark his eyelashes were as he dreamed. A distant part of me knows I should be happy it happened. But all I feel now is pain.

Because I know it won't happen again.

Ice begins to coat my skin. I hurry to my car and start the engine, which rolls over reluctantly. The clock on the dashboard reads 2:21—I can make it to the depot before the train pulls out of Kennedy, leaving me with a string of thoughts and an undocumented ache of what is and what will never be.

I drive. My grip is tight on the steering wheel, too tight, as if I might shatter without it. A tear trembles on my cheek. It splatters on my thigh. Hot. Tiny. Impossible to ignore. As the night rushes past I relive every moment: his heady sigh, his fingertips trailing up the dip in my back, his mouth against my throat. The pattern of shadows over us. Moonlight. The tangle of sheets and covers. The explosion of heat and realization and stars.

Then, without warning, another image shoves its way into my head.

Myers. Standing in front of a gravestone. One with my name on it. He's alone, in the cold, and his eyes are so hard. As if he's forgotten how to smile.

This is what I'm doing to him. To all of them.

A sob claws up, but I don't set it free. I glare at the white lines of the road as they fly toward me. In three minutes and twenty-two seconds, the sign for the trailer park appears on the right. I park next to Mom's car and cut the engine. Idiot goes wild. Snow crunches beneath my shoes as I start for the depot.

Amanda is not here. Relieved, I retrieve my cans from the office and pause by the door on my way out. There's a long window in front of the counter, with benches beneath it where people used to sit and wait for their train. My reflection stares back, but I don't even see it—I see those numbers. The shrinking days and seconds.

Uttering a loud cry, I strike out without thinking. My fist smashes through the glass, and pain blooms across my knuckles. Glass sprinkles to the cement. My chest heaves, and fire licks through my fingers and up my wrist.

At least the numbers are gone. I cradle my hand and hurry out; the train will be leaving soon. I step over the tracks, plastic bag clinking, and stand in front of a car that has lime-green graffiti of some gang name decorating the uneven surface. Bleary and broken, I stare at it for a few minutes. Thinking.

All I know is that tonight, I want to paint something that has meaning. No more empty scenery, no more insipid animals.

So I do. I am the lines that I spray, I absorb the colors and lose myself in the angles and curves. And when I finally step back, the taste of paint in my mouth, there's a girl reaching across the metal. Out of her chest there's an explosion of numbers, and her mouth is open in a silent scream.

It feels like I've given up something inside myself and put it on that car. I'm lighter and emptier, yet heavier and sadder. Ignoring the way my hand is smarting, I put the paint back under the counter and leave again. I place my feet in the prints I created on the way here. The stars whisper to me, and one of the voices sounds distinctly like Vanessa. I ignore all of them.

At home, I tiredly turn the key in the lock. Something near my foot catches my eye, though, a splash of white that doesn't belong on the dirty steps. I give the ground a cursory glance…and the world shrinks.

It rests on the step with an air of vicious innocence. Waiting for me. Taunting.

A gardenia.

Chapter Twenty-Two

On Saturday, I don't go to the lumberyard.

Instead, I drive to Karlstad.

For the past few days I've been in a strange state of numbness. There's no point in telling Allen about the gardenia, since he never saw the original one—the first one I found on Vanessa's desk.

My hair is a long braid over my shoulder and I've made an attempt at mascara and clothing that isn't sweats and a T-shirt. Boots hug my calves, my jeans are dark and clean, and my long-sleeved shirt is black and unassuming. Maybe if I don't look like the mess that I really am, the woman at the florist shop will answer more questions.

Once I get to Karlstad, however, I don't immediately head for Roses and Bouquets. No, the first stop I make is at a music store. I find the item that's been on my mind for days now, a tiny thing that shines gold—a harmonica. The clerk puts it in a paper bag for me and rings it up.

Next, I go to the pawn shop to sell the locket my father

gave me. I leave with a new wad of cash in my back pocket. It will help with all the unpaid bills sitting on our kitchen counter, and there's no point in clinging to some trinket when I won't be around to remember its significance.

I try to ignore how heavy my heart feels and get back into the car.

The flower shop is on Main Street. It's easy to spot, a colorful building right between an antique store and a pharmacy. The sign is a handmade confection of curling words and bright petals. I've never been very good at parallel parking, but I try anyway. Swearing under my breath, I leave my car halfway slanted out onto the street and go inside.

The smell of flowers immediately hits me and my nostrils flare. I look around, taking in the abundance of vibrant roses and daisies and tulips. They peer from behind the glass doors, on the shelves, on the floor. My stomach flutters when I spot some gardenias in the corner.

There's a woman in plaid standing by a register. Her numbers read nine years, three months, two weeks, two days, fourteen hours, sixteen minutes, and six seconds. Gray streaks through her hair, yet there's a youthful air to the way she moves.

"Hi," the woman says, smiling fleetingly as she glances up. "What can I help you with today?" She puts some yellow roses into a glass vase. A second later she yanks the arrangement back out and sets them down, frowning severely as if the guileless flowers are to blame for her trouble.

I approach the counter, gripping the strap of my bag with pale knuckles—the cuts from last night are covered with makeup. I touch the edge of the surface to steady myself. "Hi. Are you Martha Reynolds?"

A bubble pops from her mouth, pink and sudden. I jump. "Sure am."

Although a barrage of doubts make me want to turn around and run back to my car—*she won't tell you anything, she won't remember, you just came to hear what you want to hear*—I force myself to stay where I am. "My name is Ivy. Uh, we spoke on the phone the other night. About Myers Patripski?" His name is hard to say with such casualness.

This gets her attention. "Oh, yeah." Martha continues to chew her gum as she looks me over. "You seemed pretty upset. Is everything okay?"

Once again I'm presented with the choice between truth and lie. I hesitate. Maybe it's because there's so little time above my head, or because I've done enough lying for several lifetimes, but I can't. "No," I say bluntly. "Everything isn't okay. I'm sorry, but I need to know more about the boy who came in and bought those gardenias."

Martha ties a ribbon around the rose stems, then tilts her head and once again eyes them critically. "Sorry to hear that. What do you want to know?"

My pulse is racing. "What did the boy look like?"

"Tall. Dark hair. He wore black, baggy clothes." The ribbon comes undone and she curses.

"Curly hair? Brown eyes?" I press, ignoring this.

Giving up on the roses, Martha twists her lips from side to side as she thinks. "I'm too old for this. No, not brown eyes. Blue. I remember because he had an eyebrow piercing."

Now my heart pounds with relief. For a moment all I can think is, *It's not Myers.* He'd been telling the truth about his card being stolen. The thought consumes me until others crowd in. It's not Myers, but now I'm right back where I started. There's no one with eyebrow piercings in Kennedy, or anybody that matches that description. "That's all I needed," I say to Martha, forcing a smile. "Thank you so much."

"Yeah, no problem." She's watching me with a fathomless, intent expression. Just as I reach the door she calls, "Hey, Ivy."

"Yes?"

She stands there with one hand on her hip, the pile of scattered roses in front of her. "A gardenia symbolizes secret love, did you know that?"

"No, I didn't."

Martha picks the ribbon back up, apparently ready to try again. "Maybe whoever sent you the gardenia doesn't want to be found."

Which is exactly what I'm counting on.

"Thanks again," I mumble after a second, pushing the door open. It shuts behind me. As I walk down to the car, wind frees some curls from my braid and they whip into my eyes. Gray clouds roll through the sky.

My phone rings as I'm circling the crooked car. I pull it out and glance at the screen—Myers. My breathing quickens. I can't do this, not yet. I move my thumb and press END. He doesn't leave a message, and I hate that I want him to. I shove the phone back into the dark depths of my coat pocket.

The hinges on the door moan. I get in, blowing on my fingertips to coax warmth back into them. Before heading for home, I adjust the vents toward me.

The drive feels shorter this time. It could be the cold, or the knowledge that my ex-boyfriend isn't a murderer, or the numbers glowing in the rearview mirror. Thirty-two days. December is only a couple of weeks away.

I just want to get home, where it's easier to avoid truth and timers.

I'm going through town when I remember my purchase at the music store. Changing course, I start for the north side of the train tracks. Where people like Tommy and Brent live.

After ten minutes, the Wyoming house appears through some trees—I haven't been back since the night Myers caught me and Brent together—and a lump forms in my throat. I stop next to the mailbox, the brakes squealing. Quickly, I reach over to the passenger seat and pick up the bag. I feel the tiny bulk of the harmonica inside, something I heard Shannon mention at the Halloween party. Something that might give her a small sense of peace before her time runs out, too.

Rummaging around in the glove box for a pen, I pull one out and scrawl her name on the side of the paper bag. I shove it into the mailbox, and mentally cross one more task off my list.

Both Mom's and Lorna's cars are gone when I pull into my space at home. I don't see the piece of paper until I'm outside, walking down the sidewalk. I stop, frowning.

On the front step, in the same spot where I found the gardenia, someone left a flyer for the winter formal.

Chapter Twenty-Three

The next three days are quiet.

Everyone is caught up in preparations for the dance. I visit Hallett, I drift through school, I go to work, and I sit in my room until I am just another shadow. Myers gives up on calling, but he sends me messages that I don't stop myself from reading. *We need to talk.* When I don't respond he adds, *You can't avoid me forever.*

What he doesn't know is that I don't have to avoid him forever…just for the next twenty-nine days.

The gardenia on my nightstand begins to wilt.

Mom watches me with worry in her eyes, though I can't bring myself to reassure her. It's occurred to me how impossible it is, what I'm doing. There's no right way to say goodbye. There's nothing I can do to fill the empty spaces, no way to repair the cracks in the plaster that is our lives. I could leave presents in mailboxes, I could keep trying to find the monster that leaves gardenias as a calling card, but it won't change anything—I'm still going to die. So I sit with my back to the wall, counting.

Madness hovers and waits patiently. I could succumb. Eunice's voice echoes through my mind, spatting, *The world hates me. It does, it does. Unfair, cruel, stupid world.*

But this time it isn't Eunice who turns on the light.

It's Lorna.

The clock reads 8:26 when she comes in. I cringe as the lightbulb comes to life, sending yellow rays to the floor and into my eyes. I see how ugly this room is. Lorna crosses her arms and leans against the doorjamb. Her bedroom door must be open, since I can hear music coming from her computer. The sound coils beneath my skin and hisses. I don't move or look at her. "So you're not showing up to work today?" my older sister asks when the silence stretches.

Outside, snowflakes swirl. "The diner will find a new dishwasher," I answer flatly, watching the way frost spreads across the window. They'll need to find one, anyway, when my time is up. Is that the only difference, the only dent I've made in this huge world? Some clean dishes?

Will the diner even stay open when Nick and I are gone?

"It's been three days of this mopey shit, not to mention those 'sick' days you just got over. You're freaking Mom out again. We all thought you were past being stupid and self-ish. Get up, Ivy." I turn my head and frown at her. Lorna's eyebrows come together. There's sliver glitter on her eyelids and it flashes. "You heard me," she snaps. "Get your ass off the fucking floor and go to work. You're supposed to be the strong one in this family."

The strong one. I almost laugh but the sound dies in my throat. "Graduation is coming up in a few months, you know," I tell her suddenly. It comes out soft, distant, as if it will be less real that way.

Lorna pushes away from the doorway, not so angry now. Her expression is interested. "Are you actually nervous? You?"

"Yeah," I answer, swallowing. She probably thinks I'm anxious about the ceremony or everything that comes after.

There's a pause. Wind howls, making the walls of the trailer creak. Lorna surprises me by sliding down the wall until she's sitting beside me. Our hips touch. She's wearing some kind of fruity perfume. What's the point, when she's not going anywhere? "I haven't heard you mention college applications," she says.

"I didn't fill any out."

Lorna crosses her hands at the wrists, resting them on her knees. "So, what's your plan?" she asks after eleven seconds. "Hang out in here, feel sorry for yourself, wish you could change what can't be changed?"

"The plan..." I let out a breath. "I don't have one anymore. I thought I did." My gaze falls on the darkness beneath my bed, and I think of the box. The new pictures of an orange-haired girl named Kailey Bray, who was once a college student at Crookston.

"Look, baby sister," Lorna says, bringing me back to the present. "Plans are overrated. So is tomorrow. There's only now, and what you can do with this moment." She closes her eyes. It's strange, how old she sounds.

And I won't have the chance to get any older. I smile bitterly, which she doesn't see. "You're right. Tomorrow is overrated."

Lorna reaches over and pats my shoulder. Dismissive,

patronizing. Apparently she's finished. Just like that the brief kinship between us dissolves. Studying my sister, I can feel something clicking into place. An ending. In another lifetime, maybe it would have been the beginning of something else. Not here, though. We're just two girls in a quiet room, linked by blood but nothing else. *Goodbye, Lorna.* She doesn't hear the thought, of course, but that's okay. It's enough, how close we're sitting. There may not be such a thing as the right goodbye, but there is such a thing as a good one.

Together, we watch the storm.

• • •

It starts the next morning.

A nagging sense at the back of my head, an insistent buzzing, like a fly next to my ear. I know there's something I'm forgetting. Something I need to do. I sit in class, frowning at my teachers without hearing their words. I sit alone at lunch, picking at my food and squinting in thought. I read my lines during play rehearsal without any real emotion, provoking a puzzled glance from Chuck. When my phone goes off—more messages from Myers—I turn it off with only a small, distracted twinge.

It's when I'm doing dishes at Nick's I finally remember. Realize the thing that's so important, what I've lost sight of because of all the doubt and self-pity.

Miranda.

Chapter Twenty-Four

The front doors slide open, and a gust of wind and snow follows me inside. It's late; visiting hours are far past over. Rita hangs up the phone as I get closer to the counter. Without preamble she says, "Miranda has been asking for Hannah constantly." She pauses, giving me a moment to catch my breath. "But I think she means you."

I nod, glancing at the clock on the wall. Seven minutes left. "How is she?"

The nurse sits down, reaching for her coffee. "Fading," she replies wearily. "Dr. Simonson says she doesn't have much time."

There's nothing more to say, really. I leave Rita and walk down the hall. The carpet is worn from so many people doing the same, going to the same places, to the same people. But there are always changes, too. Like tonight.

Her room is dark. A humidifier blows in the corner, a button glowing orange. The curtains are drawn, but the luminescence from the snow outside makes the pink material glow. Miranda sleeps, just a tiny lump in the bed. I lower myself into the chair I've sat in so many times before. It creaks, and Miranda stirs at the sound. Her eyes flutter open.

"Hi, Mom." The soft words are almost a shout in the stillness. Light from the hallway slants over my face.

The small woman blinks, as if I might be a dream. When I don't disappear, an answering smile spreads across her wrinkled face. "Hannah," she breathes.

I find her hand, lost among the covers. Her fingers are so frail. "I hear you're not feeling too good," I murmur. A nurse walks by.

Miranda swallows. The action looks painful. "As a matter of fact, I'm dying," she rasps. Her grip tightens. White wisps of hair hang in front of her eyes.

I've never heard anyone utter the truth aloud with such ease before. It takes me a moment to speak again. I lean forward and brush her hair away, wanting something to focus on. "Are you okay?" I ask finally, making sure my voice is even. "I mean, you're not in any pain?"

She shakes her head. "That nice doctor is taking care of me."

We don't say anything else for four minutes; I'm doing my best not to reveal how much I ache. Suddenly, as if she senses it anyway, Miranda's eyes glisten. "I'm not afraid, you know," she tells me, like it's a secret. "I never was. But...oh, honey, I don't want to leave you alone. I don't want you to be alone."

I smile through tears that come out of nowhere, blurring everything. "Don't worry. I'm not."

Miranda lets out a sigh that's so long, so pained that her entire chest deflates. She looks at me through fast-diminishing eyes. "Who do you have, Hannah? Who's going to take care of you?" She extends her index finger to my cheek, and I bend so she can touch it.

Blindly, I reach for her other hand. That strong grasp of hers is loosening, but now I hold on tight enough for the both of us. "I can take care of myself," I tell her, trying to sound firm. "I think it's time. I'm strong, you know."

"I always knew that," she mumbles. "But everyone needs someone."

"Don't worry," I say again.

It might not be the ending she wanted, exactly, but it seems to be enough. She closes her eyes. "I love you. Don't forget that."

"Never."

My friend lets her head turn to rest more fully on the pillow. "You're a good girl, Ivy."

My name on her lips is just a whisper, a dwindling fragment, but I start. "Miranda, are you..." I stop. She looks...peaceful. I've seen painful deaths, sudden deaths, violent deaths. Never did I think someone could die and do it so willingly. Welcomingly. I lean close one last time, putting my lips next to her ear. The numbers tick down. "You're going home," I whisper. "They're waiting for you. Don't be scared. Just go."

And for the last time, Miranda Raspberry smiles.

• • •

Another day passes. Another day closer to my last.

Classes are a blur. My thoughts are consumed by the image of the peaceful expression on Miranda's face, the way light and shadow quivered over her face. I don't hear the lectures as I watch the numbers around me count down.

It's hard to breathe when I pass Vanessa's decorated locker and think of the night in Havenger's Woods, remember the flower on her desk. Then I picture my own gardenia and the invitation on the step. The gloves in Mitch's room that I can do nothing about. The receipt with Myers's name on it, linking him to everything.

I'm running out of time.

Strangely enough, Amanda sits beside me in each period. It's as if she knows I'm fading. During lunch she drops her tray next to mine. She hunches over her food and eats without a word. I poke at some peaches with my fork, glancing at her now and then. Chatter surrounds us, but our table is silent.

Myers stops trying to reach me. I check my phone over and over, hoping for another text message to ignore. Nothing. This is what I wanted, isn't it?

Play rehearsal is agony. We're back on the stage. At the start of the quarter, Chuck mostly focused on the group scenes first, but as opening night for *On a Wednesday* gets closer and closer, he makes Mitch and me do our scenes more. Today I stand beneath a spotlight, trembling. All eyes are on us again. "Is this really how you want things to end?" I demand, trying to sound firm. My voice quavers, betraying me. *Did you kill all those girls?* I want to scream. Instead I add, "Is this really how you want to remember our last conversation?"

Mitch turns to me, and there are ashes in his eyes. "I don't really care, to be honest," he answers.

There's no script for me to clutch, to hold as if it's a

lifeline. "That's a lie," I counter, drawing from memory. "I know you care."

He smiles. It's a tiny, cold curve of the lips. Something in his eyes is strange and light, as if he knows something I don't. There's no trace of my old friend. "Go to hell."

Funny. Vanessa said the same thing to me once.

"And…scene!" Chuck waves from his chair in the front row. "Great job, you guys. I have no changes. The emotion coming through here is great. Really, it's great."

Before he's finished speaking, Mitch hops down into the aisle. I watch him walk away while a voice in my head insists, *Wrong. Something is wrong.* I think about the diner receipt that says he was there when Jill disappeared. The gloves that I found in his room.

But this is Mitch. A boy I grew up with, a boy who loved his sister, a boy who once teased me by tugging on my pigtails. How does that boy evolve into a ruthless killer? It doesn't make sense. None of it does.

While I'm lost in thought, Chuck dismisses us and everyone heads for the doors. With one backward glance at me, Amanda follows the crowd. She's the last one out. I put my script on the stack and slowly move to the stairs, my mind buzzing.

The lights shut off.

"Damn it," I mutter. The glow of my numbers is too faint to guide me; I can't see a thing. "Chuck? Are you there?" I call out hopefully. No answer. Bending, I put my hands out and pat around the floor, searching for the edge of a stair. One of my shoelaces is undone. I ignore it as I keep looking.

Creak.

I freeze. Straighten. Strain to see in the darkness. Rays of light stream from beneath the double doors at the far end of the auditorium, but they don't help at all. There's no glow of someone else's numbers that I can see. "Chuck? Amanda?"

Silence. Frowning, I inch forward cautiously. Forget the stairs, I'll jump down. The vast blackness of the auditorium is unnerving.

Creak.

It comes from right behind me. I halt again, heart in my throat. Terror makes time stop.

"I warned you," a voice whispers in my ear. A glow joins mine.

Instinct seizes my limbs. With a gasp, I bolt for the exit. I forget that I'm on the stage and suddenly I'm flying. I land on my stomach and elbows. Pain radiates through my bones. In an instant I scramble back to my feet, wincing, and making a beeline for the light under those doors. I trip on the dangling shoelace and fall yet again with no chance to recover; there's the sound of heavy footsteps on the stage, a rush of air, then a hand knotting in my hair and yanking back.

I scream.

He doesn't let go, and for a moment I fight, clawing and screaming and kicking. *Why doesn't anyone hear?* He pins my arms to my sides and he's strong, too strong. I pause to catch my breath and then I remember the seconds over my head. A bizarre calm fills me.

It isn't time yet.

"What do you want?" I breathe, my chest heaving. Adrenaline is already leaving me, and fresh pain sets in.

He doesn't answer. His breath heats my ear. He holds me away from him so I can't tell if he's tall or short or heavy or thin. For ten seconds we stand like that, as if we're a statue forever connected. *Twist around, look at his numbers!* sense shrieks. But I can't move.

The silence becomes too long. I snap. "*What do you want?*" The screech bounces off the walls and echoes.

Three more seconds go by. *One. Two. Three.* "I want to let you live," he rasps.

And he lets me go.

Chapter Twenty-Five

I don't tell Allen. I don't tell anyone.

Instead, I leave the auditorium, get in my car, and head to work.

Then, after a long shift, I go home. As I pull up behind Mom, my side aches from the fall. Her taillights fade to nothing, and while I'm parking she gets out. Idiot barks. Mom waves at me as she walks up the stairs and pulls the screen door open, huddling in her coat like a turtle. Plumes of air leave my mouth as I hurry to catch up.

The sound of Spencer Hille greeting us drifts through the trailer. For once, I don't have a retort ready for the parrot. Mom immediately goes to her room to change out of her greasy uniform. I just sit in the closest chair, which happens to be in our chaotic kitchen. There's a tiny window over the sink, and through the creeping layer of frost on the glass, I notice there are no stars—just more darkness.

To fill the time and occupy my thoughts, I catch up on homework there's no point in doing. Mom takes her laptop out into the living room and curls up in a blanket, a space heater at her feet. Minutes or hours pass; I'm not sure which. Eventually my stomach rumbles, so I get up and warm a Pop-Tart. I sit back down. The simplicity of it all makes me feel better and worse at the same time.

Crumbs scatter across my notebook when I take another bite. Abruptly frustrated, I slam the textbook shut and shove the chair away from the table. The legs squeal against the floor. Mom doesn't even blink. Pop-Tart in hand, I start down the hall toward my room like I always do, but falter at the sound of Mom coughing. Lorna is holed up in her room again, probably doing her show—the glow from her computer slips beneath the door.

Tonight, I don't want to be alone. So I turn, stride back into the living room, and plop down on the couch beside Mom. After a moment, I nestle into her side. She reeks of the diner, and her elbow digs into my side, but I don't move. "Pop-Tart?" I offer quietly.

"No, thanks," she says, and I know she didn't even hear me. Surprisingly, she doesn't move away. She probably doesn't have the energy. She sits there and stares at her laptop with distant eyes. The whiteness from the screen spreads across her face, and as I really look at her, I realize how haggard and old she's gotten. She's still beautiful to me.

Then, finally, I feel the sting of tears in my eyes. I want to tell my mom everything. About the sleepwalking, the attack, Miranda's death. All the rest. But I can't bring myself to ruin this moment. Unable to look at her anymore, I adjust my head and watch the words come to life beneath her hands. I could ask her what she's writing about, but part of me doesn't want to. I'd like to think she's writing some happy story.

I'd like to think she's rewriting mine.

• • •

Madonna sings me awake again.

I put my glasses on and squint at the clock. The red numbers blur and focus. We're late. I throw the covers aside and leave the warmth of my bed. It's so cold I can feel the floor through the carpet. "Mom!" Rushing to her door on tiptoe, I pound on the wood. It rattles. "Get up! Nick is going to kill you!"

Madonna restarts her chorus for "Material Girl." "What's the point of working for your brother if you can't sleep in?" Mom shouts back. I picture her burrowing deeper into the pillow.

"Don't make me come in there!"

Mom grumbles something too muffled to catch. I reach for the knob and falter. She needs to do this by herself. Starting now. "I'm getting dressed!" I say through the door. "If you're not up, you're on your own!"

She doesn't bother with a reply. Blinking rapidly, I run back to my room. I wriggle out of my sweats and hoodie. I yank on the first things I see, which turn out to be some wrinkled jeans and a red turtleneck. My glance happens to flit past the mirror mid-yank, though, and I pause. Lift the shirt up higher to reveal my ribs. They're black and blue— it must have happened at some point in the auditorium.

The memory is hazy now. What I remember most, like a neon sign, are those words: *I want to let you live.*

I could show this to Allen, I think, trying to stay calm and detached. *He'd believe me then.* But what would I tell him? Someone attacked me in the dark? That I saw and know nothing, really, besides that the killer must be male? Which they've already concluded on their own.

I pull my shirt back down; Allen would only dismiss it as another prank. He doesn't want to listen to anything I have to say. With one last, harried look at the clock, I leave my room.

Mom is in the bathroom, thank God. Using the sink at the same time as the shower makes the water cold, so I grab my toothbrush and go into the kitchen. The faucet starts with a sputter. As I brush, I notice some mail beside the sink. Spitting, I flip the light on and pick up the first envelope. It's from the power company.

Mom appears, out of breath as she ties her wet hair back. She sees the bill in my hand. "I'm going to pay that," she sighs. "Next paycheck. Aren't you eating breakfast?"

Food is the last thing I want right now. Putting the bill down, I shake my head and shove all my books into a backpack. "Have a good day, Mom," I say and kiss her cheek. She gives me a puzzled smile, and I know it's because I've been so affectionate lately. I just turn my back and leave the trailer.

"Later, gorgeous!" Spencer Hille shouts.

I go straight to school. I can't seem to go back to Hallett yet. Ice gleams in the parking lot and I grimace as I fight for balance; every movement makes my ribs twinge. Besides that, the day is like any other. Astronomy and English. Chalkboards and droning voices and pencils scratching over paper. It feels as if there's a balloon inside me, expanding and expanding with nowhere to go. I stare out the window and wonder if he's watching. Waiting. But he had his chance, didn't he?

Then I remember the invitation in the snow.

The lunch bell rings. Same food, same table. Amanda doesn't show up today. Seated by the trash bins, I watch Mitch Donovan and all his friends and wonder. Was it him in the auditorium?

He must feel the heat of my silent accusations, because he lifts his head and stares back at me. He smiles the strange, little smile he had yesterday in rehearsal. Shuddering, I tear my gaze away from Mitch and concentrate on the piece of bread in my hands. I begin to tear it up into little pieces and arrange them on my lunch tray. There's no real design or purpose to it. Once the bread is thoroughly destroyed, I open my milk and pour it onto the pieces. I watch the bread swell as it soaks.

The school counselor, Mr. Pepper, walks toward me. He's smiling, and when he stops the smell of his cologne assails my senses. He's wearing pants that are too tight and there's a stud in his left ear, as if he's trying to be one of us. Except people stopped wearing those sometime in the nineties. "Hi, Ivy," he greets me. "How are you?" He notices my tray and the bizarre mess I've made. His smile slowly fades.

"Fine," I say. For good measure, I pop a chunk of the now-soggy bread in my mouth. Nausea claws up my throat.

Mr. Pepper purses his lips. "Ivy…"

"I have a lot of homework to do, Mr. Pepper." But

the textbook beside me is closed, untouched, and we both know it.

The counselor's brow is furrowed in concern now. "You can talk to me anytime," he says. His voice is firm, as if he doesn't think I believe it. "And it doesn't even have to involve Vanessa. You can talk about anything."

I just nod, and Mr. Pepper leaves with a hesitant smile.

Suddenly I can't sit here another second.

Feeling Mitch's eyes on me, I stand, dump my tray, and go in search of the other lonely girl in Kennedy.

Chapter Twenty-Six

Amanda sits on a bench in front of the school, smoking a cigarette.

I knew this is where she would be—it's one of the few quiet places, the empty places. We both seem to be drawn to those. That and I already checked everywhere else. I sit beside her, rubbing my arms. "You'll get in trouble if you're caught," I mumble.

She blows a long stream of smoke out. Her hair hangs in front of her face. "So?"

A van goes by. The mayor's wife, Carol. Her head swivels in our direction and I catch her eyes narrowing. I give her a cheerful smile and a wave. Once she's gone, I take a breath and angle my body toward Amanda. She doesn't move; she continues squinting up at the afternoon sun. She almost looks pretty. Not so angry. "I heard some girls talking in the hall today," I say offhandedly. "They said you live with old lady Biscoe?"

Still no reaction. "What about it?" Another inhale. Hollows deepen in her cheeks.

I shrug. "Well, she's just never taken a kid in before. Mostly she sits on her porch swing and yells at anyone who steps on her lawn."

A bitter smile turns up the corners of Amanda's mouth now. "Guess the old lady needed some money," she tells the sun. "Biscoe got certified as a foster parent a few months ago."

"Oh. I hadn't heard that." I shift on the bench.

Amanda looks at me. The orange tip of her cigarette crumbles. Ashes fall. "That's because you don't pay much attention." There's obviously a double meaning to the words, and I think of the starry night we met. *Don't you care that I might be about to die?*

You won't.

Already my limbs are stiff with cold. I fall silent and consider my next words. Amanda reaches up to grip her cigarette again, and her sleeve slips a little. Her cuts stand out starkly against our pale surroundings. I swallow, and I can't look the other way today. With each passing day, hour, minute, second, it's clear that time won't stop just because I have. Hearts will continue to beat and wings will continue to flap. The train will still speed down the tracks and the snow will melt. So finally I ask, "Why do you do that to yourself?"

"Do what?"

I level a look at her, and Amanda suddenly glowers as she understands. She tugs at her sleeves. "It's none of your business," she snarls.

Her ferocity doesn't intimidate me—not when I only

have twenty-six days left. "Maybe it is," I counter. "As bad as it sounds, I've been so distracted with everything that's going on in my life that I haven't really taken you seriously. But, Amanda, you thought about *killing* yourself. You hurt yourself."

As swiftly as she's alive with fury, Amanda shuts down. She slumps and takes another drag. "I'm not looking for pity." A cloud moves in front of the sun, and the world fades to gray.

The right words are hard and impossible. So I say what I'm thinking. "Pity, no. Someone to notice, though? Maybe."

She throws the cigarette stump to the ground and smashes it with the heel of her shoe. She glares at me as she does it. "If you tell anyone—"

"Don't bother. Threats don't work on me."

The new girl cocks her head. "You're that cold, huh?"

Watching the timer over her greasy dreadlocks, I swallow. "No, I'm just a little different from most people." And for once, it doesn't bother me to admit it.

Before Amanda can respond, my phone rings, and I don't need to look at the screen to know who's calling. My traitorous heart leaps as I pull it out and check. His name makes my blood quicken. But I still silence it.

Amanda appraises me. "What do you want, exactly?" she snaps when our gazes meet.

I shove Myers back into my pocket. "I want you to talk to someone besides me. That's it. Someone who can help."

Her expression darkens. "No one can help."

"You're going to be alive for a long time," I say bluntly. "Do you really want to spend those years existing instead of living?" *You're one to talk,* a little voice sneers.

There's another pause. Inside, the bell rings. Time to go back to class. Amanda scowls, and the moment I see that, I know she'll agree. "You're a pain in the ass, you know that?"

The clouds suddenly part again, and rays of light touch the ground. "I think we could have been good friends," I say with a faint smile, standing. Amanda doesn't follow suit. "Well…see you later."

"I know what you're doing."

Frowning, I face her again. "What do you mean?"

Without warning, Amanda pulls up her sleeve to reveal those angry, crimson cuts. It's so unexpected, when until now she only hid them. She raises an eyebrow at me, and her eyes are bright in the weak sun. "It takes one to know one," she says. "Your wounds just don't show."

She'll never realize how right she is. Amanda Ryan is surprisingly perceptive. "Don't forget," I say as an answer. "Talk to someone. Anyone."

"Who will you talk to?" she calls while I'm walking away.

It makes me falter, for just a moment. But then I know. *Who will you talk to?*

Who I always talk to.

• • •

The angels weep.

I'm standing in front of a gate. The rusting design is all swirls of black iron. Pillars on either side hold stone angels, their arms and wings straining against them as if to escape. Their expressions are anguished and broken.

I haven't been back to the graveyard since the day of the funeral.

My boots crunch in the snow. I push the rusted gate open and my mind goes back to that awful day. During the entire ceremony I'd just stood there behind her family, as stony as the angels trapped in those columns. Her mother openly wept, her father looked a moment away from hitting someone, and Mitch didn't take his eyes off the ground. There were dirty looks from those who believed I was guilty of something, but Uncle Nick's arm around my shoulder and my own numbness shielded me from it all. The pastor went on and on and I didn't hear a single word.

Afterward, everyone trickled out of the cemetery. Even her family. Mom, Nick, Susie, and Amar seemed to make some kind of silent agreement—they left me alone with my best friend. She was just a waxen shell, lying there in that dark, closed casket. I looked down at it, shivering. There were no thoughts. No words. Only death and solidarity. Then the quiet was shattered by the soft *thump, thump, thump* as the diggers shoveled clumps of dirt on her.

I don't know how long I stood there. Long enough that the sun began to sink below the horizon.

The same way it sinks now. I glance at the orange skyline. Vanessa's grave is under a big, old oak. The bare branches struggle to stretch over her, protect her. As I get closer I see that someone has been here recently; there's a half-frozen rose. I kneel, looking around at her new home. The stone next to hers simply reads, HOW TERRIBLE IT IS TO LOVE SOMETHING THAT DEATH CAN TOUCH.

I always wonder if the person who said those words saw the numbers, too.

My best friend waits. The silence grows unbearable, and I force myself to speak. "Hey, Nessa." My voice comes out hoarse, and I clear my throat. Her gravestone stares back at me. I purse my lips against the tight sensation inside me. Rising, smothering. "I don't really know what to say. Maybe there's too much. Maybe there's nothing, really. I always wonder if you can hear us. Watch us. Guess I'll find out soon enough."

A tear hovers on the end of my nose and I swipe at it. Wind whistles through the emptiness. "Do you want to know the most horrible thing about all of this? I mean, besides knowing when everyone is going to die? It was not being able to tell you. I just couldn't. You wouldn't have believed me anyway."

The hinges on the gate whine. I jerk toward it, and feel my eyes widen at the sight of Vanessa's mother, Rachel Donovan, weaving through the headstones. Her head is down; she hasn't seen me yet. A wool scarf obscures half her face. Quickly, I leave Vanessa's grave and hide behind the small mausoleum a few yards away. I leave tracks in the snow and silently hope that Rachel won't notice.

She doesn't—she only has eyes for her daughter. The last time I saw her was months ago, in the frozen food aisle of the grocery store. I'd been too afraid to face her, to watch her expression change until she looked at me the same way Mitch does. So I left. I regret it in this moment, watching her.

Rachel stands in the spot I've just vacated. For a minute there's nothing but silence and cold. Then she exhales. "The house is so lonely without you," she murmurs, running her gloved hand along the top of the slab as if it's the curve of

Vanessa's cheek. The breeze carries the words to me. "Mitch is never around and your dad works all the time. Sometimes I watch the front door, thinking you're going to be home from school any minute." Rachel presses that hand to her mouth now. A muffled sound drifts through the air. The dead sleep on.

My instincts are torn. Part of me wants to go to her, to take away her pain. Another part cowers. Ashamed. If Mitch is convinced of my guilt, what do Vanessa's parents think? In all the time since her death, they haven't said a word.

In the end, I leave Rachel in the same state as the moment she entered the graveyard: alone.

And the angels keep on weeping.

Chapter Twenty-Seven

"Do you want to go to the winter formal with me?"

Brent Nordstrom says it so no one else will hear, but my head still snaps up as if he's screamed. He must see the instant denial in my eyes. Hastily he adds, "Just as friends."

At this, I hesitate. We're in English class and everyone has chosen partners to work with on a project. Mitch and his friends sit in the back corner beside the windows. Amanda is next to me, and I know that even if she seems enthralled by the assignment, she's listening to us. "Why?" I ask Brent after a long pause.

He glances over his shoulder. His jaw tightens as I watch him make some internal decision. Without invitation he settles into the desk on my other side. The chair creaks. He's too big for it, really. His arms bulge out of the sleeves of his T-shirt. "Would you believe me if I told you it's because I want to?"

"No."

Sighing, Brent glances at Amanda, who swiftly looks

back down at the paper in front of her. I roll my eyes and lean closer to Brent. He has a white-knuckled grip on the edge of my table, as if without it, I might float away. "I want to keep an eye on you," he mutters. I know he's telling the truth this time. "It's Mitch. He's out of control."

"I can't really stay away from him, Brent. We're in the play together. He's still obsessed?" My stomach clenches.

The teacher gives Brent a pointed look as she walks by. He smiles charmingly, then focuses on me again. "Obsessed?" he echoes. "No. Convinced you had something to do with Vanessa's death? Definitely. I guess my dad was asking him about some evidence you found? I don't know the details, but it only pissed Mitch off more."

There's a flash, a mental image of the light beneath the auditorium doors. It comes back, the sensation of someone yanking me back by my hair. The faint glow of numbers I couldn't see. A voice in my ear. *I want to let you live.* Now it doesn't seem like a calculated attack, but a burst of fury.

My gaze meets Brent's. His earnestness makes me want to tell him about the gloves and what happened in the auditorium. And ask if there's a possibility it was Mitch. Before I can he says slowly, "So will you? Go with me, I mean?"

Another pause. Brent's numbers stare back at me. Thirty-seven years, eight months, two weeks, seventeen hours, fifty-two minutes, and six seconds. Uncle Nick may die trying to save me, but Brent has a life ahead of him. Keeping him by my side wouldn't harm anything. Maybe it buys me more time, should the killer attack during the formal. Maybe I don't have to do this alone.

Miranda's voice sounds in my head. *Everyone needs someone.*

"Oh, just go with the poor kid," Amanda snaps.

I shoot her a halfhearted glare. Then, facing Brent again, I take a breath and say, "Okay."

"Okay?" he repeats, as if he isn't sure he's heard correctly. I nod, gather up my books, and go to the door. Amanda and Brent frown in confusion—class isn't over. "Hey, where are you going?" he demands. Guess he wasn't kidding about protecting me.

"There's something I need to do." I tell them before bending to murmur an excuse in Ms. Jones's ear. She nods. Eyes bore into my back as I leave the room. I take a right, another right, and walk down the hallway. The office I'm looking for isn't hard to find; there's a piece of paper next to the door that reads SCHOOL COUNSELOR. There was once something written beneath it, but it's been scribbled out.

I falter in the doorway. "Mr. Pepper?"

He's sitting behind a tiny desk, and the surface is littered with folders. At the sound of my voice he raises his head so swiftly it looks painful. "Ivy. Hi!" he chirps. "Come in. Please." He gestures to a chair against the wall opposite him. The office is tiny and his cologne is overwhelming. I bite my lip to stop myself from asking him to open the window.

"You said I could talk to you about anything," I say as I settle into the chair.

The counselor beams. There's so much gel in his hair it looks fake. "That's right, I did. I'm glad you took it to heart."

I let out a breath. "Okay. I want to talk to you about Amanda Ryan."

He blinks.

• • •

"You're my best friend. What am I supposed to do without you?" Shannon asks me, tearful.

Most of the props are finished, so I look up at her from a hospital bed today. The sheets are scratchy. "You move on," I rasp in answer. The lights are so bright, nearly blinding.

Suddenly Chuck stands, his brow puckered. "Hey, can you guys pause for a second?" My head is turned toward him already and Shannon looks over with a scowl. Chuck just rubs his bearded chin. "Thanks. Uh, I wanted to remind you that this is a last conversation between two best friends. You know what that means, don't you? Someone you know better than you know yourself. Someone you would do anything for. *Someone you can't imagine losing.* I need more…emotion here. Shannon, you look like you've swallowed a moldy grape. Could you try something else?"

Her nostrils flare as an answer.

Chuck opens his mouth, but the bell rings before he can utter one more word. I'm the first one off the stage and heading for the door. Everyone else follows at a more leisurely pace. I wait in the hall, leaning casually against the lockers, and watch each face as they pass. *Did you do it? How about you? Are you the one?* When Mitch walks by, he doesn't even notice me. Maybe I really am fading into nothing.

My skin crawls when Chuck turns off the lights. I must move, let out a breath, something, because he suddenly realizes I'm standing there. "Oh. Hi, Ivy." He puts the script into a bag dangling off his burly shoulder and turns. "Did you have a question?"

I don't, really. But I find myself thinking of the words he's written, of the story he's created. And somehow I hear myself asking him, "Do you believe in heaven, Chuck?"

The teacher makes a gesture for me to walk with him. He's so tall his head nearly brushes the ceiling. Kids give him a wide berth. "I believe in something after death," he answers after a moment. "Something more. Heaven? Maybe. Not sure I buy the pearly gates or choruses of angels, though." At this, I smile a little. Chuck grins back. "Why do you ask?"

We pass Vanessa's locker. One of the poems has fallen to the ground, an old piece of tape beside it. I step on the words, *We'll never forget you.* "Just thinking about what happens to Emily after the goodbyes, is all," I say lightly. We're in front of his classroom now. I hear the slow hum of a harmonica—it has to be Shannon, showing off for her friends—drift through the walls. The sound is bittersweet.

Chuck's expression alters somehow at my response, but I can't tell what he's thinking. For a moment the man just regards me, his hand on the doorknob. I fidget with the ends of my too-long sleeves. Finally he says, "I'd like to imagine she'll be at peace."

This makes me pause. *Peace.* There's that concept again, the sensation so far out of reach. It must be real, because people like Miranda and Chuck seem to believe in it. But the only thing I utterly trust are the numbers. And what kind of peace can be found in that?

When I let the silence linger too long, my teacher opens the door. "See you tomorrow, Ivy."

"Chuck?" I blurt. He pauses, eyebrows raised. My voice is soft as I ask, "What was her name?"

The bell rings. We're out of time. But Chuck doesn't rush or seem offended at the question. Instead, his eyes become distant as he remembers. "It was Danielle." A common one, but made beautiful by the way he says it. With one last, sad smile in my direction, Chuck ducks inside and closes the door.

And I think of Myers.

Chapter Twenty-Eight

Mom's typing echoes in my ears. Tonight it makes concentrating on homework impossible, but while I would normally retreat to my room, I don't. Not now, when there's so little time left. I push back from the kitchen table. Mom sits on the couch again, squinting at her computer screen. The space heater hums at her feet. "Do you want something to drink?" I call to her, creaking into the kitchen. She doesn't answer. We're out of bottled water, so I reach up and take a cup out of the cupboard, then to hold it beneath the faucet as I twist the handle.

Nothing comes out. I twist the other handle. Still nothing. My hand forms into a fist, and I press it against the edge of the counter, slamming the cup down. *Damn it, damn it, damn it.* Mom must have forgotten to pay the bill. Or just couldn't. None of us will be able to take showers tomorrow. I'll have to call the company in the morning to see if anything can be done. I lift my head, suddenly so, so tired, and catch my reflection in the window above the sink. I look older.

Ironic, since I only have twenty-five days left.

Mom sits there, completely oblivious. I know she's trying, but I can't stand the idea of leaving her like this. There has to be something I can change. One thing I can do.

As I stand in the stale-smelling kitchen, an idea comes to me.

Nearly seventeen minutes later Mom tears her attention away from the computer. She turns that squint on me, and it takes her a few seconds to speak. "What are you doing?" Her tone is baffled.

Bottles clink in the garbage bag I'm holding. I bend to pick up a beer can off the floor and shove it in with the others. "Cleaning."

There's a line between her eyebrows, as if she doesn't understand. "Why?"

Straightening, I put the bulging bag next to the garbage and grab a new one off the counter. I shove my hand inside and snap it in the air three times. "Because it needs to be done." The mountain of dishes in the sink will have to wait until the water is turned back on, though.

Mom continues to watch me with a perplexed frown. Finally, slowly, she stands. The blanket on her lap falls to the floor. "Okay," she says. "Okay. I'll help you."

"Great. Vacuum is in the hall closet. Dust rag is on the shelf above it. Knock yourself out."

Silence. I feel her eyes on me as she turns. She walks away, and the floor marks each step. Soon there's the sound of a door opening, and a *thud*. She's really bringing the vacuum out. But there isn't the familiar whine of the vacuum wheels. Instead, Mom takes two more steps, and she knocks on Lorna's bedroom door. My sister says something that I don't catch. Hinges groan. "Hey," I hear Mom say. "Get your ass out here. We're cleaning."

"We're *what?*"

Exactly two and a half hours later the trailer is unrecognizable. The garbage is gone and the table gleams. All the scattered papers and piles of junk in the living room have been taken out, too, and the carpet smells fresh. The suspicious mold in the bathroom shower has been scrubbed away to reveal the white plastic beneath; we got inventive with some of the supplies under the sink, since there's no water to work with. And Spencer Hille hops around in his newly-cleaned cage. "I love you!" he announces.

"Yeah, you're welcome, stupid bird," Lorna mutters. She's squatting in front of the fridge. Mom assigned her the unpleasant task of taking everything out and sniffing it. Suffice to say, we'll be going grocery shopping.

Mom stands in the middle of the living room, surveying it all with her hands on her hips. The curtains around the window flutter; we opened it to let the stuffy smell out. "Not bad," she says, brushing a wisp of hair out of her eye.

Walking up behind my mother, I tuck my head in the curve between her neck and shoulder. Lavender shampoo teases my senses. "It looks great, Mom." She pats my cheek absently. After a moment I say, "I'm going to bed. 'Night." She mumbles something unintelligible as she eyes the smudged windows. Once Mom sinks her teeth into something, she doesn't relent. She's going to be okay. She is.

She doesn't see me slip away.

I brush my teeth with just the toothpaste, take off

my glasses, put on some boxers, and lie down. But I don't sleep. An hour goes by. It feels as if I'm about to do something—take a test, run a marathon, jump off a cliff. My heart pounds and my entire body tingles. The numbers on the clock mock me by slowing down.

Then I hear it. *Tap. Tap. Tap.*

This time I recognize the sound. Not Mom's keyboard, not the click of Lorna's fan or Spencer Hille picking at the bars of his cage. Maybe I've been waiting for it. I put my glasses back on and pad to the window on tiptoe. It resists just for a moment. I lean out, crossing my arms over my chest. The sight of him makes me feel like a dozen people at once, all raging to be free of this single body. "Myers, I…"

His eyes burn, and the words die in my throat. "You didn't exactly give me a choice," he says quietly. "You wouldn't answer any of my texts or calls."

"Most people would take that as a hint." My tone is sharp, but suddenly all I can think about is how cute he looks in that stocking hat.

Myers glowers. "Just let me in. I can't feel my face."

I step back. "Can you ever feel your face?"

He wraps his hands around the sill. "Good point." He hauls himself inside. As usual, he's so much more graceful than I am. And then he's standing here, in my room, not a figment of my dreams anymore. His curls wrap around the edge of his hat, and the tip of his nose is red. He smells like frost and gasoline. Somehow, it's a rousing combination. He's wearing the coat I gave him. Why didn't he get rid of that when we broke up? Why keep it all this time, wear it?

I don't know what to say. But Myers does. "You think I don't see what you're trying to do, Ivy?" he asks quietly, glancing toward the door. The words are feather-light, but they have the force of bullets.

Wincing, I concentrate on his chest so I don't have to look into his eyes anymore. "I'm not doing anything," I mumble, and wish I were a better liar around him.

He moves closer. "You're pushing me away. And I'm not going to let it happen again."

I swallow. "It isn't up to you, Myers."

"The hell it isn't."

Now I lift my gaze to meet his. I see our last night together in his eyes, and it takes everything I have not to flinch, not to close the breath of space between us. "Ginger likes you," I whisper, reminding myself more than him. "You slept with her. Did you forget that?" I try to be angry. I try to find a way to hate him again. All I can do, though, is hurt and wish some more.

Myers doesn't back down. A muscle works in his jaw, and the moonlight slanting over him makes his pain that much more palpable. "No. I haven't," he answers. "But I also haven't forgotten this." He raises his hand. I tense, expecting him to touch me, to destroy what resolve I have left with the heat of his fingers. Instead, he gives me his phone.

Frowning, I look down at the image on the screen. I click to the next one. My mind doesn't want to accept them at first. It's undeniable; these pictures are exactly what I think they are. I shake my head, clenching the phone tight. "These…How did you…"

"I started going to the tracks ever since that picture was sent to me. You know the one." He smiles a little.

Blushing, I hand the phone back to him. "That was over a year ago." It's the only response I can come up with.

Without invitation, Myers moves past me to sit on my bed. Springs squeak. "Yeah. I never went to the depot—I know that's your place—so I didn't tell you. And after you cheated on me, I tried to stop. I wanted to forget you but I couldn't. So every Friday night I go watch the train pass and take pictures of whatever you've done. I can always tell which ones are yours. They're the most beautiful." His voice changes, from that simmering anger to something infinitely sad.

I stare at him. Really stare. For the first time, I see how much he's changed. What I've done to him. There are bags under his eyes and they're red-rimmed. He looks pale, thin, tired. It's as if I put a spell on him, and no matter what I do, he can't break free of it. "I didn't know. I had no idea," I say. How can I fix this?

Do you want to? that vicious little voice asks me.

Myers takes a breath, like he's about to dive into freezing waters. He closes his eyes for a moment, then opens them and looks directly at me. "I'm ready."

I blink. I'm still standing in front of him, fidgeting uncertainly. "Ready for what?"

His expression hardens. "Ready to listen. Tell me why. I want to know what made you give us up. What your reasons were the night you kissed Brent. Maybe it's unimportant, considering everything else that happened that night. But I need to hear it."

It's so unexpected, so blunt that I falter. Slowly, I sit beside him. It seems we're destined to have all our meaningful conversations in night-shrouded bedrooms. As the silence lengthens and I keep hoping he'll take it back, it becomes apparent he's going to wait for me to answer. Finally I make a helpless gesture. "There were a hundred reasons, Myers," I whisper. "I'm not used to boys wanting me. Maybe I was just curious. Or too drunk to say no. Maybe I wanted to ruin us." The last part makes my heart ache. Because I know it's true.

His hands become fists at his sides. I hate myself for being the cause of all his misery. "Why?" he rasps. "*Why?*" Once again his sorrow swiftly turns to anger, the cold darkness of his eyes giving way to a bright, searing heat.

Because I thought it would make things easier for you. Because I love you. Because it seemed like the only way. "It doesn't matter, really, does it?" I ask him, focusing on a stain on the wall. "We can't go back. Time doesn't work that way."

When I turn toward Myers, he's frowning. "You're always talking about time. What do you know that I don't, Ivy?"

Alarms go off in my head. I'm saying too much. I don't want Myers anywhere near me on the day it happens, and if he suspected, nothing would keep him away. He may not die, but I won't let him watch. "I know that it's late," I reply after a pause that's too full, too long. "And you should go home. Thank you for showing those pictures to me. It means a lot. Probably more than you know." I attempt a smile.

Myers rubs a knuckle in his eye, and the leather watch on his wrist slides down his arm. "Ivy—"

"You should be with Ginger." Part of me means it.

He closes his mouth and just looks at me. There's nothing in his expression now, not fury or sorrow. There's only a sort of detached observation. This time I know what he's going to say before he says it: "This isn't over, Ivy."

I stand, pretending my heart isn't breaking all over again. "It has to be." I go to the window.

The wind greets me when I push the frame up. I shiver, cupping my elbows, and raise my eyebrows at Myers. He doesn't put up a fight. With one last glance at my face, he drops to the ground. Then he's a shadow, running through the night. I shut the window and strain to see him until the last possible moment. I press my palm to it, aching. "Goodbye," I whisper. The word is acid and poison and everything fatal.

Even after he's gone I let my fingers linger on the glass, until the cold creeps under my skin and into my bones. Maybe if it goes deep enough, it will numb everything.

As numb as death.

Chapter Twenty-Nine

On the morning of the winter formal, I visit Russell at Hallett Cottages again.

This time there are no poetry books, no stories, no teasing. I enter his room and it's completely dark. The curtains are drawn over the window. Hesitantly, I turn on the lamp and turn. He lies there, hands folded over his chest. His eyes are open and he stares at the opposite wall. It's almost as if he's waiting.

I skirt around the bed and sit in my usual spot. He doesn't react. Tufts of hair stick up around his ears, and his blue eyes see something that I can't. "Are you all right?" I ask.

Russell lets out the smallest of sighs. He turns his head to look at me. "I'm old," he answers. "I'm dying. Sometimes you just need a moment."

"A moment for what?" I ask, though I already know.

He feebly waves his hand through the air. "To remember." His expression softens. "I've led a good life. I'm ready to go."

"Ready," I echo, my voice barely a whisper. Envy curls in my stomach. Maybe it's something that comes with age, or it just happens. But I'm not ready. Not even close.

I lean forward, resting my elbows on my knees, and think about the box under my bed. Russell watches me now, strangely patient. "I've been looking for someone," I say, feeling a line between my eyebrows deepen. "And every time I think I might find him, something goes wrong."

The old man doesn't ask questions. He thinks. Then, slowly, he tells me, "Usually the answers we're looking for are right in front of us. And sometimes we see what we want to see." He sounds so tired. His eyelids look heavy, as if his eyelashes are made of steel. *He's not fighting it anymore*, I realize. What must that be like, to stop fighting?

Then I think of Miranda, and I know. It's peaceful.

Which is something I don't have the luxury of, at least not yet. I take a breath, leaning forward again to make him focus. "I'll let you rest, but there's one more thing."

Russell nods. "Shoot."

Guilt assails me now. I don't let it hinder me. *Nine days left.* "I've been thinking about doing something," I murmur. Down the hall, a phone rings. "Something that could be cruel. But in the end, it might do good."

"Was there a question in there somewhere?"

I sigh. "You know what I'm asking, Russell. Should I do it? Is it right?"

Outside, the sun brightens. The room glows with blue light as it struggles to shine through the curtains. Russell meets my gaze, and he seems more like the man I've known all this time. There's a knowing shadow in his eyes, and past all the wrinkles and frail bones, the vibrant young man he used to be still exists. "There's a big difference between what's right for you and what's right for someone else," he answers. His tone is suddenly brusque. "I'm not a shrink or a priest, girl. And you already know what you're going to do, or you wouldn't be so torn up about it."

As usual, he's right. Smiling, I flatten my hands on my thighs and push myself up. "See you later, old man."

"Go to school and learn something," he grumbles.

At the doorway, I pause. The fluorescent lights in the hallway beam down on me as I look back at him. Russell hasn't moved. He's watching me go. Studying him for what will probably be the last time, I bite my lip. The numbers over him tick down from the three months he has left. I won't be there to see him off.

An old woman rolls by in a wheelchair and gives me an odd look. It jars me back to reality. Facing Russell again, I clear my throat. If there's one thing, one truth I can give him before we both leave the world forever, it's this. "If I could have chosen my father, Russell, I would have picked you."

He doesn't say anything. He doesn't have to; he blinks rapidly. I want to stay, I want to listen to another one of his stories. But I can feel time working against me and I have to go. For the last time, I smile at Russell Montgomery.

Then I leave.

When I get to my car I flip the rearview mirror down and pinch some life back into my cheeks. The engine starts, whining about the cold, and I head for school.

As soon as I step through the double doors, though, I don't go to my locker or to class. Instead, I walk to the computer lab, a tiny room adjacent to the library. Absorbing the smell of old books and the plastic of new computers, I scan the room, the faces behind each screen. The one I'm looking for is tucked away in a back corner, hunched over his keyboard as if someone might snatch it away at any second. Without hesitation I start toward him with Russell's words going around and around my head. *There's a big difference between what's right for you and what's right for someone else.* The boy sees me coming, and his eyes watch my progress while his fingers never stop typing.

Theodore Hicker. But everyone calls him Ted the Hacker.

I reach his side and don't waste time. "I need you to get into a site."

He avoids my eyes. He looks younger than he is, with his tiny wrists and too-big shirts. "What's in it for me?"

Wordlessly, I put a wad of cash on the desk. Everything that I got for pawning the locket. There's a part of me—no, more than part of me—that knows I should give the money to Mom. But this is more important than electricity.

Ted looks at it for two seconds, then lifts his head to meet my gaze.

"What do you want me to do?"

• • •

My hands shake. As I attempt to apply some eyeliner, I keep glancing at my numbers in the mirror. It's bizarre that tonight, they're a reassurance. They mean that whoever is coming to the winter formal won't succeed in killing me.

Just for tonight. *You can do this*, I tell the pallid, frightened girl looking back from the glass. *You've survived worse.*

She doesn't look reassured.

"Is that Brent Nordstrom's car?"

Mom's voice travels through the entire trailer. The eyeliner pen clatters to the counter, and I hurry down the hall. Mom stands in front of the window, gaping. "Oh, God, don't—" I begin.

Lorna's voice comes from behind, startling me. "Hold it," she says. "What the hell is *that*?"

I turn to face her, and follow the direction of her wide eyes. "It's a dress," I mumble, shifting from foot to foot. It's the only one I have, the one I wore to Vanessa's funeral. It's black, short-sleeved, and stops at my knees.

My sister shakes her head. "No. Uh-uh. That is not a dress. That is a *catastrophe*. Come here. Right now," she adds more forcefully when I don't move. But then we all hear the sound of the screen door hinges. *Knock. Knock. Knock.* I halt, opening my mouth. "Let Mom get it," Lorna hisses. Our mother is already reaching for the doorknob. Meekly, I follow Lorna into her room.

"Hi!" I hear Mom say. If either of them thinks it's strange I'm going to the winter formal with Vanessa's boyfriend, they're not saying anything.

Lorna shuts the door and goes straight to the closet. I stand uncertainly, clutching at the bottom of my dress. "After what you did to my black swan costume, I shouldn't let you anywhere near my clothes," she mutters. She shoves some shirts down the metal bar. Hangers clatter. "But I can't let you go out in public like that. I just can't. Where is it…" She yanks out something in plastic casing and drapes it over the bed, smiling.

It's pretty. It's pale green and glitters with beads. Something a mermaid might wear. I can't even bring myself to touch it. "Where did you get this?" I ask.

She's bent toward the floor, probably looking for the shoes to go with it. "Are you forgetting that I went to high school too? This is what I wore to my senior prom. I went with Bill Moody." She shudders. "He works at the gas station now. And he's going bald. I dodged a bullet there."

"Doesn't he have an account on your site?" I ask distractedly, unzipping the protector.

"What are you waiting for? Try it on!" She puts her hands on her hips and glares now. There's a shoe in each hand. Heels, I note with a sinking sensation in my stomach.

"I don't know. I don't think I can pull it off," I say, edging toward the door. Really, I just want to avoid putting those things on my feet.

Brent is saying something; the low rumble of his voice drifts down the hall. Mom responds. Ignoring them, Lorna snatches up the dress and holds it out for me. "Look, Ivy. I know you've been through a lot in the past year. Which is why you deserve this. So put on the fucking dress, and go have fun for a change." She shakes it for emphasis.

Still I hesitate. If something goes wrong tonight, that dress will definitely slow me down. "I'm not you, Lorna," I argue, searching for a legitimate excuse. "Boys don't look at me and fall all over themselves. This dress is for that girl."

She rolls her eyes. "You're looking at this all wrong, Ivy." Dropping the dress back on the bed, Lorna grabs my shoulders and guides me to the wall-length mirror beside her desk. Reluctantly, I look at myself again. For once I manage to ignore the numbers. "You have amazing hair," she snaps, as if it's so obvious. "Great skin. A beautiful smile, when you actually use it. Okay, you're tall. And okay, you have no boobs to speak of. But I know at least one boy who likes all of that." She gives me a knowing look that could rival Russell's.

My skin grows warm, thinking of Myers. "He's not coming," I tell our reflections. Even to my own ears, it sounds sulky.

"Then don't do this for him. Do it for yourself."

We're wasting time. "Fine," I say through my teeth, pretending as if my stomach isn't doing flips inside of me.

Spencer Hille squawks from the kitchen. At least he cares that I'm late. Lorna nods, like she knew I would agree to this all along. "Now, we need to do something about your makeup and your hair. Jesus, Ivy, don't you know *anything* about being a girl?"

Ten minutes later I emerge from my sister's room. A third person has joined the group in the living room—Uncle Nick stands beside Mom. He winks at me, and Mom's eyes are suspiciously moist. It's so strange. She's never exactly been maternal. "Oh, honey," she says softly. "You look beautiful."

For some reason, I'm unable to look in Brent's direction. "Thanks for seeing us off, Uncle Nick," I say, rubbing my arm self-consciously.

"You're gorgeous, kid."

"Thanks," I repeat. I can't avoid Brent any longer. When I turn to face him, I see that his smile is different than Mom's. It resembles mine: something bittersweet, trapped in the past and the present. We're both thinking about Vanessa.

You look fabulous, bitch, she would have said, looping her arm through mine.

It shouldn't be this way. But it is.

I tilt my head back and look up at Brent. He's trying to hide his own sorrow, but I know. Mutely, he puts out a corsage he'd been holding behind his back. It's white. Like a gardenia. My family watches as I present my wrist and hide a grimace. The band snaps into place, sealing the flower against my skin. It won't last long, but that hardly matters.

The knowledge whispers through me. *Eight days.*

Brent helps with my coat. Bored, Lorna wanders back to her room before we leave. I wish I could hide in her closet. Brent gets the front door, and I step over the place where the gardenia and invitation were left. We descend the steps and he hurries to open his car door for me. I turn back to smile at Mom and Uncle Nick before ducking in. He wraps one arm around her shoulders, and she uses her free hand to wave. My date gets in, buckles, shifts gears, and reverses. My family stays on the front step until we drive out of sight.

The silence is so loud. I sit in Lorna's dress, feeling like I'm wearing a disguise or another costume. *You can do this, you can do this,* I keep mentally chanting. Brent grips the steering wheel tightly, staring out into the night. He looks as nervous as I feel. "Ready?" he finally asks. The word trembles in the stillness.

"Yes," I lie.

The car picks up speed. "Then let's go to our winter formal."

Chapter Thirty

The gym has been completely transformed.

Paper snowflakes dangle from the ceiling, and the walls are covered in aluminum foil. A disco ball spins and sends light in every direction. Pop music vibrates through the wooden floor. All of this combined with the brightness of everyone's numbers is disorienting, and I stop where I am, blinking.

A hand touches my elbow. "Are you all right?" Brent says in my ear. In the chaos of it all I'd almost forgotten he was here. I nod, glancing around at each face. My classmates laugh and talk and dance. Teeth glint, dresses sparkle, jewelry flashes. Teachers stand on the sidelines looking on. "Do you need something to drink?" Brent shouts over the chaos. I just nod again, and his warmth disappears. I keep skimming the crowd. Looking for whoever wrote that message in the snow. Wondering who left the gardenia and the note. I move along the outskirts of the room, ignoring the scattered glares and speculative mutters. The long skirt of

Lorna's dress drags behind me. My heels click against the hard floor. The music suddenly changes into something soft and vulnerable.

Where are you?

"Ivy."

I'd know that voice anywhere, and I hurriedly look over my shoulder. There he is, the disco lights dancing across his dark eyes. The first thing I notice is the tux. Sleek, black, overwhelming. But I forget about this when I look at his face—he hasn't shaved in a while and stubble shadows his jaw.

"Myers, how did you—"

"Dance with me?" He doesn't wait for a response; he just takes me in his arms and guides us onto the floor.

My feet automatically fall into the steps. I know I should stop this, go look for Brent, but I can't bring myself to. "What are you doing here?" I manage, clutching Myers's hand so tightly it must hurt. He smells good. God, I want to forget myself in him again.

His chin rests against my temple. Myers is one of the few people in this universe who make me feel delicate, breakable, beautiful. As an answer to my question Myers whispers, "Maybe it's cliché, but the moment I knew I was in love with you, you were standing across the room. In the middle of a conversation with Vanessa, probably. You turned your head, looked at me, and smiled. I couldn't breathe."

The gentle sound of a piano echoes through the hot, glittering air. The room is dim and the crowd so thick that it's easy to hide the sting of my tears. "Why are you telling me this?" I ask evenly.

His hold on me tightens, and I don't think he's even

aware of it. "Because that feeling never went away, Ivy," he says doggedly. "You destroyed me when you kissed Brent. Vanessa's murder changed you. And then I made everything more complicated by getting involved with Ginger. The point is, we have so many reasons to give up. But when I start thinking there's no way it could ever work, I remember that day."

My stomach flutters, and I start to answer. A familiar face in the crowd catches my eye, though, and my mouth closes. There's Brent. He's standing on the sidelines, holding two drinks in his hands with an anxious expression. He hasn't seen us yet.

Eight days left. My fingers are loose and it's as if Myers knows he's losing me; he brings me closer, closer, until our lips are nearly touching. Everyone around us fades away. "How?" I ask, but it's not a question. I know how this will end. It's a plea. I am Miranda. I am Emily. In this moment, I want the lies and the happy endings.

He smiles, reaching up to brush a curl off my forehead. "One day at a time."

If only it were that simple. "A lot can change in a day, Myers."

"Not everything," he counters. "Not the way I feel about you."

Brent is coming this way. People see his approach and begin to whisper again. I see their lips shape the words. *He came here with her? How could he? Traitor.* He stops right beside me, his expression neutral, and Myers stiffens. Seeing that, fresh regret sears through me. The two of them used to be friends. That drunken kiss between Brent and me ruined multiple relationships that night. "Myers," Brent says coolly. Suddenly I remember the morning he showed up to school with a black eye. It was after everything happened. I never asked him about it; I didn't need to.

My ex-boyfriend's eyes narrow. "Brent."

"Can I cut in?" the other boy asks, offering his hand.

Myers finally releases me. I still feel the imprint of his hands, hot spots under my skin. He retreats with a thunderous expression. He thinks there's hope where there is none. Brent puts his arms around me, but it isn't the same. Not even close. I watch Myers walk away over Brent's shoulder. He looks back, just once. And then he's gone.

Silence settles around us. Brent's hold is strangely tight. Is he really that afraid? "I don't see Mitch," I say finally.

"Maybe he'll be a no-show," Brent replies. He doesn't sound optimistic, though. If he had any idea—if he knew of the very real threat I face—I'm not sure he would be here.

For a few minutes we sway back and forth, saying nothing. It will never feel right, being with the guy Vanessa loved. Being with the guy I used to push Myers away. But something has changed between us; he's more than Vanessa's boyfriend now. Maybe not all changes are bad.

Ironically, this is the moment I choose to notice that his hand is rougher than it should be. He's still wearing the bandage he had on the night he came to find me behind the diner. I stare at it and wonder how he got hurt. Football season is over, after all.

Then, in a burst of illumination, Mom's voice echoes through my head. *At breakfast one of the deputies let slip that his girl might have managed to bite whoever did it.* My mouth goes dry. It can't be. It's impossible. Yet I still hear myself asking unevenly, "What happened to your hand, Brent?"

He glances at it with raised brows, as if he'd forgotten all about it. "Cut it slicing vegetables for my mom. It was pretty deep. No stitches, though."

Just as the music changes again, there's a buzzing sound. Brent steps back and digs around in his pocket. He pulls out a phone, presses a button. He frowns at the small screen. "I got a text from Mitch," he says. "He says he's with Allen and they need to talk to me. I guess they're out in the hallway."

We move off the dance floor. "Should I go with you?" I ask him. My voice is stiff.

Oblivious to this, Brent shakes his head and pockets the phone again. "No. Just stay here." With long-legged strides, he heads for the same doorway Myers disappeared through. He ducks under the silver arch.

I shuffle to the back of the gym, wincing because of the pain radiating from my feet. My mind whirls with thoughts about bites and bandages. But it could just be a coincidence. Brent *adored* Vanessa.

I find an empty chair and take off the heels. Damn Lorna, I should've worn my sneakers. The clock over the wall says it's only quarter past seven—it's going to be a long night. What if the flyer was random? This could all be for nothing.

No, not for nothing. I need to get a look under Brent's bandage.

My own phone, tucked in the space between my non-existent breasts, goes off. Glancing around to make sure no one is looking, I pull it out and open the text, yearning to see Myers's name. The combination of anguish and anticipation dies when I see it's from Brent. *Meet me in the boys' locker room. Now.* My heart quickens. Did Allen finally find something? Does he believe me about the note or the gloves? Is it about Jill? I stand so quickly that I trip on my skirt. Impatiently I yank it up and rush, barefoot, out of the gym. I can feel the stares.

The locker room is at the back of the school—everyone always complains that it's too far from the gym. Just another Kennedy High oddity. I run through the shadowed hallways until I see a doorway at the end with gold letters above it. BOYS. *Something isn't right,* instinct suddenly whispers. I understand the need for privacy, yet this doesn't feel right.

But it's Brent, logic argues.

Brent with the mysterious bandage on his hand.

Reassured by the fact that I still have time over my head, I pull on the handle and go inside. There's an unmistakable male scent in the air. "Brent? Allen?" My feet make slapping sounds against the tiled floor. I let go of my dress and glance around the darkened room. The lockers stare back with slits for eyes. I'm just about to spin and run when I see it.

A shoe on the ground. Black. Shining.

It feels as if I'm walking through tar. My steps are slow, hesitant, dreading. I round the corner. The shoe is attached to a foot. He's shoved up against the lockers, and his eyes are closed. His chest is barely moving. "Brent?" I whisper, horrified.

"Nice dress," a voice says behind me.

I open my mouth to scream, but a hand clamps down on me and muffles the sound. I start to struggle against a hard chest and two wires for arms, still trying to shriek. An instant later a sweet-smelling cloth smothers everything. I feel my eyes flutter and I fight it. The edges of the room turn to black. It all tilts.

Then fades completely.

• • •

"How much did you put on it?"

"Not that much, okay? She should be waking up soon."

"If you killed her, I swear to God I'm not going down for this, Jeff!"

"Jesus, would you relax—"

"Guys. Shut up. She's coming around."

My world returns slowly. Faces. Trees. Ice. Cold. I realize that I'm lying in the snow and looking up at Mitch Donovan. The silky dress is soaked—Lorna is going to kill me. Mitch stands with his feet apart, arms crossed. His expression is anger and hate and pain. Two of his friends hover, and it's obvious they're not as certain as he is. Moonlight shines down on all of us, making this scene seem entirely surreal. But I know I'm not sleepwalking or dreaming.

"You. You were the one who left me that invitation," I slur. Mitch doesn't answer, and I remember what happened in the locker room. The sight of Brent's still foot. Right now, the bandage on Brent's hand doesn't feel important. I sit up and the world tilts. "What d-did you do to him?"

"Brent will be fine," Mitch says shortly. "We just used a little chloroform. It's you I would be worried about."

I manage to stand on trembling legs. I'm still barefoot.

My skin prickles and burns. "What are you going to do?" I ask Mitch, trying to sound strong. Unafraid. Instead I sound young and terrified. My throat is on fire.

His jaw clenches. White clouds mark each one of his breaths. "I'm going to leave you out here. In the cold," he hisses. "Alone. Just like you left Vanessa. Don't think planting some stupid gloves in my room is going to save you."

"Mitch—"

"Give me your phone." He stares at me, waiting. I think about lying, but then I remember getting that text from Brent. Of course the real sender was Mitch. Seeing no other way, I take the phone out of my dress and hand it to him. Without hesitation he whirls and whips his arm at a tree trunk. Plastic shatters against the bark. Mitch faces me again, and his chest heaves as if the effort took everything from him. Or maybe the real effort is restraining himself, containing all of the fury inside. Suddenly I don't see someone angry and vengeful anymore; I see a sad, broken boy who lost his sister too soon. Those words he screamed at me in the diner—*You could have saved her*—have a whole new meaning.

A strange calm fills me. And my voice, when I speak, is a shiver of strength. "I don't know who killed her, Mitch, and I would've saved her if I could. I know you would've, too."

Something in his eyes flickers just the tiniest bit. Doubt. But after three seconds he turns his back on me. "Let's go," he mutters. My heart sinks.

Surprisingly, Jeff doesn't move. He glances at my toes, peeking out from beneath the ruined mermaid dress. "Look, man, we can't just—"

"Get in the fucking car, or I'll leave you here, too."

The headlights of his SUV flash as Mitch unlocks the door. The boys climb in, but Jeff hesitates again. They're really leaving. Fumbling, Jeff takes his shoes off and throws them in my direction. He doesn't look at me, and I don't thank him. I just pick them up, shaking off the slush, and put them on. It hurts. The hard material rubs against my raw skin. They're too big, of course. But they're shoes.

The engine whines to life and Jeff shuts the door. The headlights blind me for an instant as they swing away. I stand in the green dress and the huge shoes, helpless to stop them. The red taillights smirk at me, shrinking down the road. Then darkness.

The quiet is a scream, white noise, an endless roar. Coughing, I cup my elbows and grapple with panic. I don't know what to do, I don't know what to do. The trees and the stars are cold spectators. I shiver, wishing the glow of my numbers was brighter. The thought jars me from this daze—*the numbers.* They're proof that I'm going to get through this and I'll see morning.

Encouraged, just a little, I start walking. The snow crunches with each step and the branches above cast intricate shadows to the smooth blanket of white that is the ground. I know I must be in Havenger's; the white bark of the trees is a signature. Not to mention that Mitch wants to punish me for what happened to Vanessa, and this is where she died. Which means I'm twelve miles outside of town.

This is where she died. I've been so caught up in the cold and the walk that somehow I didn't even think about it. Now that the knowledge is there, though, I can't stop it. My mind goes back, and I remember the last time I ever spoke to my best friend.

The night rushes past as I break every speed limit in the county. My cell phone is pressed to my ear so hard the feeling has gone out of it. It rings over and over. I know she won't pick up; she sees it's me. But she doesn't know that this is it. Her time is almost up. I have to hear her voice, I have to tell her—

"Stop calling me, Ivy. I don't want to see you, I don't want to talk to you."

Elation rips through me, followed by desperation. "Vanessa, please, listen to me. Take your insulin. I'm on my way—"

"Leave me alone."

Click.

A twig snaps.

It wasn't me who caused the sound. It echoes, bringing me back to this freezing, petrifying reality. I halt so suddenly that I stumble. My eyes are wide and my heart slams against the walls of my chest. I turn, straining to see in the darkness. Clouds have moved in front of the moon. I scan my surroundings again and again. Trees. Black. Bushes. Snow. Icicles. Then…a shadow moves behind a cluster of small, thin trees. *Someone else is out here.* And I know, as certainly as I know Vanessa is dead, that it's him. I clench my fists and try to find some semblance of courage within me. There isn't any.

"I see you!" I shout, my voice breaking. "I know you're there!" The shadow darts between two trees. Moving closer. Stalking. Hunting. I hesitate a beat longer.

Then I run.

My panting and my heartbeat and the thunder in my ears drowns out all other sound. If he's coming after me, I can't tell. One of the shoes falls off. I pump my arms and run faster. Someone is heaving breathy sobs—it takes a few seconds to realize it's me. An instant later, I also notice that I'm leaving tracks. What can I do? Circle and confuse him? What if he's right behind me? Tears freeze on my cheeks as I stop and plunge into a thicket of pine trees. The needles are so overgrown there's almost no snow on the ground. They reach for my face and leave burning scratches and cuts. I run and run and run. My bare foot shrieks at me. Doesn't matter, doesn't matter.

Finally, when I'm so deep in the grove that it feels safe to stop, I press my back to a tree. Struggle to breathe. I don't move, don't look, don't blink, don't even think. I listen.

Nothing.

Snow falls from a branch, and I jump. The night whispers to me, filling my mind with doubts. There was a shadow, in the shape of a man. Wasn't there? *But why would someone be out here?*

The answer comes a second later. *For me.*

One thing is certain—Mitch Donovan is definitely not the killer. And neither is Brent. I'm still going over the moment in my head, seeing that man-shaped shadow, when I hear another sound. This one is different from the others, and it makes me dizzy with disbelief.

A car.

Fear keeps me plastered there, until the distant noise of the engine begins to fade. They're leaving! Finally, I bolt. A pinecone bites into the sole of my foot as I shove branches out of the way. *Is he following, is he coming?* my terror screams. I dare to twist and look over my shoulder. I nearly fall again when I see him, unmistakable this time. His face is concealed by shadow, but he's tall. Muscled. A thick branch stretches in front of his face and his numbers.

But he isn't moving. The tree line breaks, and there's the road! The stars continue to watch as I trip and scream up to frost-covered pavement. The truck isn't as far ahead as I thought it would be—I can still make out two people through the back window. "Wait!" I cry, waving my arms frantically. "Please, *wait!*"

The brakes squeal, and before the vehicle is fully stopped I'm yanking at the door handle, clawing to get in. It opens. Shannon Wyoming, dressed in pink finery, gawks at me. The formal. They're just getting back from the formal.

"Ivy? Is that you?" Tommy frowns in the driver's seat.

Shannon cries out indignantly when I scramble over her, tumbling into the back seat. Melted snow quivers on the leather upholstery. "Yes!" I screech, cowering low. "Just drive!"

Over Shannon's unintelligible protests, Tommy faces forward and steps on the gas. The heaters are going full blast, coaxing life back into my body. Swallowing, I press my hands to the window and stare into the shadows of the trees. Wondering if one of them is him. "You're crazy," Shannon mutters to Tommy. "Look at her. She's missing a freaking shoe." I barely hear her.

Havenger's Woods disappears into the darkness.

Chapter Thirty-One

It's morning by the time I walk through the front door, and the sun stretches its orange and pink fingers across the sky. Behind me I can hear Shannon's voice rise and fall from the truck; Tommy might regret his kindness before the day is over, if he doesn't already. I don't linger to watch them pull away.

The door closes with a thunderous echo. The bottom of the mermaid dress is ragged, torn, soaking. My hair clings to my neck in wet strands, and the cuts from the pine needles sting. My foot has lost most of its feeling. All I'm capable of thinking about is a shower—hopefully the water is back on. I shuffle past the kitchen, so dazed that I don't see her. At the last second Spencer Hille calls, "Hello, beautiful!"

I hear my sister mutter back, "You have a hideous voice."

Sluggishly, I turn back. Her head is on the table. She's dressed in one of the outfits for her show, if it can be called an outfit—it's a configuration of black lace and garters.

I lower myself into the chair beside her, breathing hard. Every part of me aches. I just want to fall into my bed and sleep.

"Lorna?"

Her voice is empty. She doesn't move. "It's gone. All of it."

"What is?" I ask, though I already know. Guilt adds to the weight bearing down on me.

Her hand is a fist. I see it flex as she strives for control. "My site. It's completely crashed. I called a guy, and I guess there's no saving it. I have to start over. But I don't have the money." She finally lifts her head and looks at me. Her eyes widen. "Jesus, what happened to you?"

"Just a prank," I answer dismissively. Lorna doesn't look convinced. She opens her mouth. Before she can ask any questions I hurry to say, "What are you going to do?"

It's an indication of her distress that the weak distraction works. She doesn't even comment on the dress. Lorna laughs and shakes her head. "Guess I'm heading back to the diner until I can save up enough to get the site running again." Mascara smears out of the corners of her eyes. For the first time, my sister doesn't care about beauty.

I put my palm on her wrist. Her skin is so hot. Or maybe mine is too cold. Lorna's lips tremble at the touch, but she doesn't pull free. I consider the words before I say them. "I know it doesn't feel like it," I tell my sister slowly, "but maybe losing your site is the beginning of something. Not the ending."

She jerks away and swipes roughly at her nose. "I don't want to work in that diner for the rest of my life, Ivy!"

"Then don't," I say simply. "Just do *something*, Lorna.

You were the one who made me leave my room. I think it's time you try it, too." She doesn't say anything now, and I slide out of the chair to kneel next to her. I ignore how much the movement hurts and tenderly tuck Lorna's hair behind her ear. "I know making plans seems terrifying. I do. But if we don't make plans, what's the point of having time?"

She shudders, looking more lost than I've ever seen her. It's a good thing, I tell myself. Because it's usually when people are lost that they find themselves.

I realize she's speaking again. "...the hell did you get so wise?"

Using the table for support, I push myself up. The whole thing shakes. "When I realized I had no choice." I smile to make the statement seem hollow. She takes in my disheveled appearance again, and opens her mouth to ask questions I can't—won't—answer.

An earsplitting noise rips through the entire trailer, something akin to a smoke detector going off. There's a yelp, then a *thud*. "What the *fuck* is that?" Mom thunders.

Lorna gives me a quizzical look. My smile becomes genuine now. "I bought her another alarm clock."

• • •

November is forever a thing of the past, and December is here in all its solemnity.

It's Wednesday morning and I only have a few days left. Mom frowns in her sleep. I lie next to her on my side, willing the daylight to stay away. But it slowly leaks through the blanket over the window. Her alarm will go off any second now. *Wake up*, it will shriek. *No*, I want to say. It's warm here, and it smells like it did when I was five: lavender and sweat. It's a cocoon I never want to leave.

Maybe Mom feels the intensity of my focus. Because somehow, for the first time in years, her eyes open all on their own. There are brown flecks in her irises that I've never noticed before.

"What are you doing?" she croaks.

At first I don't answer. The pressure of responsibility tries to push its way in. I should visit Hallett. I should go to school. But then I think of Mitch's unwavering glares during class and play rehearsal, Brent's guilty apologies for not protecting me at the winter formal, the thoughtful way Amanda has been watching me, Vanessa's decorated locker. "Don't go to work today," I whisper.

A sleepy smile turns up the corners of Mom's mouth. She reaches up and touches my nose. "No arguments here," she whispers back. And she goes back to sleep.

Uncle Nick will be irritated. Susie will be on her own for the breakfast crowd. Chuck will be mad that I missed one of the last rehearsals for his play. None of it matters. I nestle deeper into the sheets, tucking my hand under my chin, and join her in dreams. It's so easy.

We wake to the sound of Mom's cell phone ringing. She mutters and rolls over. I take the phone from the night-stand and squint at the screen. Nick. I turn it off and put it in the drawer, then lie there and stare at the ceiling for a minute. My head lolls to the left, until I'm looking at the ridge of Mom's ear peeking out of the covers. "Are you awake?" I ask.

It takes her a few seconds to reply. Finally I get a muffled, "Yeah." She still sounds groggy. Awake, nonetheless.

Sunlight streams in the room, making it impossible for me to go back to sleep. I sit up on my elbows. "Let's do something. Go somewhere," I urge. Suddenly the idea is all-consuming. *Let's do something worth remembering*, I want to say.

My mother doesn't comment on the strangeness of it all. Instead, she rolls back over. Studies me. I wonder what she sees. Eventually she just says, "Okay." She brushes a hair out of my face, an unexpected gesture of tenderness. "We're going to make your sister come, too," she adds.

Surprisingly, Lorna doesn't resist the prospect. When I tap on her door and say we're going out, she just lifts her head from the mattress and gives me a bleary, empty look. Her computer sits in the corner, untouched. It's missing its usual hum. "Give me twenty minutes," she drones. I close her door, knowing I'll give her a lot more than that.

It's a day of the bizarre and the astonishing, because somehow all of us are ready in an hour and a half. The water is back on, for now. Mom looks relaxed in jeans and a button-up shirt. Lorna is more covered than I've ever seen her in leggings and a long sweater. I'm in my usual jeans and hoodie. Spencer Hille calls a goodbye just as we're shutting the door.

"Where do you want to go?" Mom asks, adjusting the rearview mirror. "We could go bowling, we could drive to the movie theater…"

I glance into the back seat in case my sister has some input. But Lorna's head is turned away. She remains silent.

"Bowling sounds fun," I say. Mom nods and turns on the blinker.

Carl Blue, Mayor Blue's father, owns the bowling alley. Since everyone in Kennedy has places to be during the day, like work or school or glued to a computer, there's really no point to his place being open so early. But for years he's opened anyway. No one really knows why.

To say he looks surprised to have customers walk through the door in the middle of the day—the Ericksons, no less—would be putting it lightly.

"Hi, Annie," he blurts, adjusting his glasses. "Lorna. Ivy. What are you ladies up to?"

"Hi, Carl." Mom slides a bill across the counter. "We're just taking a day off. Three pairs, please. Ivy, what size are you?" She glances down at my shoes. It's the first time she's ever asked me that, for any article of clothing. For a moment I just stare at her blankly.

"Nine," I tell her.

"We have the same feet, huh?" Mom nods at Carl, who's already reaching for them. She's completely unaware of the way I'm pursing my lips, trying not to fall apart. It's so unfair, that she's seeing me now. Learning about me now. Now, when it's too late.

"Why don't you get me a beer, too," Mom adds. Carl turns around and takes one out of the tiny refrigerator behind him. He puts it down in front of her. Condensation rolls down the brown glass.

Each of us takes our shoes—Mom's ring clinks against the beer in her grip—and we go to the first lane. Carl bends and switches on the lights. Colors, red and green and blue, quiver over everything. Music comes on, too, something that sounds like it's from the eighties. I make a valiant effort to pull myself together. Lorna sits down in one of the plastic chairs, toying with the ends of her hair. As Mom types our names into the system I pick up a ball, place my fingers into the holes, and face her. "Let's see what you've got, old lady."

Her eyes narrow. "Better watch what you say, little girl."

"Or what?" I ask with raised brows. Lorna's mouth twitches. Mom doesn't respond, and without another word I whirl. The ball flies from my hand. It takes six seconds. Gutter.

Mom laughs, then takes a sip from her bottle to hide the sound. I glare at her and get another ball. This time it takes down seven pins. Satisfied, I sit down beside Lorna.

Our mother is already striding past us. "I'll show you how it's really done." She chooses a ball and holds it in front of her face. She takes her time lining up the shot. We watch her arm lower and swing. It rolls, crashes through the center of the pins, and all of them fall. "Oh!" Mom shouts, pointing at me. "Who's old now, huh? Would an old lady be able to do that?"

Lorna is up next. She picks up a ball that seems too heavy for her. But my sister is stronger than anyone thinks. With little difficulty she hauls it up against her chest, lines up, and runs. She releases the ball low. *Thud.* It rolls down, down, down the lane. She doesn't even watch as it collides with the pins and each one tumbles. Mom and I clap and cheer. Lorna sits and turns her face away. Not before I see a hint, the fragile beginnings, of a smile.

We stay for two hours. Mom downs six more beers. We throw ball after ball and hit pin after pin. Shout after shout.

Carl sits behind his counter with a newspaper. Every once in a while he glances up with a grin. Finally our time runs out. On our way out the door I wave to Carl, who beams.

It's a bright afternoon. Sunny, but cold. I huddle in my coat as we return to the car. "Should we go home, my girls?" Coming up from behind, Mom wraps her arms around both me and Lorna. Her breath reeks of beer, and she giggles when I wrinkle my nose. We're halfway across the parking lot now.

"Yeah, I'm driving." Lorna takes the keys from her.

"Shotgun!" Mom shouts.

I shove her and start to run. She seizes the back of my shirt and stumbles past me. "Cheater!" I shriek. I'm smiling so hard it hurts. I let her sprint ahead. When she reaches the car Mom seizes the door handle triumphantly, and I've never seen her so carefree. So young. So alive. It's a moment I wish I could capture forever, with a camera or a can of paint. Lorna strides past me, her hair lifting in the breeze. Her head is tilted, and her lips are pursed in reflection as she absently jangles the keys. She doesn't look so lost or unhappy now.

We all load back into the car, Lorna behind the wheel this time. We head for home. Mom is talking about her book, something she's never really shared with us before. "It's about a woman who thinks her life is over. She's getting a divorce, she's unhappy at her job, her children are grown and distant. But then, one day, the daughter she gave up for adoption thirty years ago shows up on her doorstep." As she speaks she waves her hand through the air with drunken exaggeration.

"It sounds great, Mom," Lorna says.

I rest my head against the window and stare at the landscape rushing past. Their murmured conversation fills my ears, a lullaby.

I've never thought about bucket lists. I never considered what memorable, significant thing I wanted to do before I die.

But this day was it.

Chapter Thirty-Two

"So Saturday night is the big play, huh?" Susie stacks plates next to me.

A bubble floats into the air and I trail its progress up, up toward the ceiling. It pops. "Yeah, sure is," I say.

Susie pats my cheek. Her red lipstick is smeared on her teeth. "You'll do great. And we'll all be there to support you, front and center." She winks and sashays away. Her pony-tail—bleach blonde today—swings against her uniform.

It's Thursday already. What they say about time passing by more slowly if you pay attention isn't true; it still flies. In two days, after my first and only performance in Chuck's play, I will die. My grip tightens on the dishrag and I scrub a pan harder.

The hours pass. Customers come and go. I'm safe in the kitchen, where I can't hear all the typical gossip or feel the speculative looks. I bus tables and mop messes and do more dishes. Amar sings and steam hisses from his pans. There's something comforting about the routine.

"Hey, Ivy," Amar says at one point. I look up at him. He's so dear, with his hairnet and grease-covered apron. "Did you know that when an elephant dies, the rest of its herd will bury it together? It's their way of saying goodbye." He grins.

I smile back. As always, I say, "Keep the fun facts coming, Amar." This time, though, there's something broken in my voice. Our fry cook doesn't seem to hear it and I'm glad. It's a perfect last night for me and him.

At the end of the shift, when everyone has left, Mom flips the sign in the window to CLOSED. We all start work on cleanup. Amar and Susie banter back and forth. I take the bin out and head for the biggest booth. But suddenly I stop in the middle of the floor, looking around with a tight sensation in my middle. This place is more familiar to me than any other. Its age shows; the stuffing in the booth benches is coming out. The floor is so scuffed it's nearly colorless. The walls are covered with photographs, posters, signatures, quotes, a guitar that Uncle Nick once played in the band that was supposed to get him out of Kennedy.

This is where I took my first steps. This is where I broke my arm. This is where I watched Mom cry in Uncle Nick's arms when she found out Dad was leaving.

Broom in hand, Susie goes to the jukebox and finds the same song she turns on every other night. "Cowboy Take Me Away" by the Dixie Chicks. Her search for the perfect man is probably why she's been married five times. Amar winces as the music starts and he bends over a burner, rubbing hard enough to drown the lyrics out. Mom walks from table to table, refilling the ketchup and mustard bottles. While they're distracted, I wander away. The door to the office is open a crack and light spills onto the floor. I knock on the door, head in. "Uncle Nick?"

As usual, he's sitting behind the desk. At the sound of my voice, he lifts his head. "Yeah." He pulls the cigarette out of his mouth and his fingers stop typing for a moment.

I clear my throat and take a couple steps inside the room. "Amar says the stove has been acting funny. Maybe you should take a look."

He nods and keeps punching receipts. "I'll check it in a little bit."

"Okay." I turn to go, but then I pause. I turn back around. Uncle Nick glances up again and smiles when he sees I'm still there. Before he can say anything, I ask, "Will you make me...kind of a strange promise, Uncle Nick?" The brief sense of contentment from the day we went bowling is gone, leaving turmoil in its place. Sorrow, resentment, pain. There are still too many goodbyes I haven't said yet. It's so much harder when I look at his numbers again.

He doesn't even hesitate. "Anything, kid."

I know it's no use. I know there's no point. But if I don't try, I'll regret it until the second I die. So I take a breath and say it. "On Saturday, after the play...don't come and find me, okay?"

My uncle is frowning now, but he doesn't ask any questions. Maybe he sees the wretchedness in my eyes, or the desperate need. The silent scream. "Okay," he says simply.

I nod, pursing my lips. I study him as he sits there, memorizing his features, the details of this tiny room he's worked in my entire life. The wallpaper is yellowed and peeling. His chair is too small and it looks like it's going to snap in two any moment. He's wearing a wool sweater, what he constantly wears in the winter, with the sleeves shoved up to his elbows. There's scruff lining his square jaw, and his nails are chewed short.

Just like mine.

"I love you, you know," I add.

He laughs. Something flickers in his gaze. "Why do I feel like you're saying goodbye, Ivy?"

"Guess I'm feeling sentimental," I reply lightly, forcing a smile. My chin wobbles. He doesn't see it—no one sees what they don't want to see.

The thought strikes another chord within me, and I picture Russell.

"Well, I love you, too. Always have, always will. Now get going. You're distracting me."

I laugh, a watery sound. Uncle Nick is already lost in his own world of numbers. He pushes the buttons on a calculator as if it's his sole purpose in life. I leave him there, wondering if I'll have one more chance to speak to him, before the very end.

Somehow, I don't think so.

• • •

Midnight rolls around, and I'm still awake. I lie motionless in bed, with one arm over my head. The plastic stars on the ceiling stare down at me. *Two days*, they whisper. As if I could forget. Every noise is heightened. Lorna's fan, Mom's clacking on the keyboard. I can't stand another moment of it, so I reach for my glasses and get up. The constant *tap-*

tap-tap from Mom's room guides me through the darkness. I push her door open and lean against the frame.

She doesn't react to my entrance. She just keeps writing. Mom is wearing a nightgown that looks like it belonged to Grandma, with a scoop neckline and lace on the trims. Purple flowers dot the threadbare material. Her feet are bare and propped up on the space heater. Somehow she found the time to paint her toenails red. "What are you doing up?" she mumbles distractedly, the glow from the screen illuminating the line between her eyebrows. *Tap-tap-tap*.

"Can I talk to you?"

"Of course, honey." *Tap-tap-tap*.

Taking a breath, I walk to her bed and sit. The movement causes the mattress to bump the nightstand, which in turn makes the beads on the lamp quiver. I watch light quiver through the glass as I say, "I've been thinking."

"About what?"

It's so hard to say. This is supposed to be a time of irresponsibility and rebellion; being born with the numbers made me even more so. But I've always been different. Which is why here, now, I must say it. "I think that you need to pack up Dad's stuff. All of it." I shift my gaze from the beads and focus on her. Wait.

The typing stops.

For a moment, Mom doesn't move or speak. After six seconds she leans her elbow on the back of the chair and angles her body toward me. She keeps her gaze on the floor, though. Because if she looks at me, she won't be able to avoid this. "Where did that come from?" she asks. Her voice is distant.

I'm holding the edge of my T-shirt so tightly I can feel

my nails through it. Involuntarily, I remember my mom ripping a picture of him in half, tears running down her cheeks. "We need to stop pretending," I say. "We need to face everything while we still have time."

Her fingers twitch. I know that all she wants right now is to twist back to the computer and go back to her perfect world. Her better world. "Face what, Ivy?" she asks next, making an obvious effort to sound normal.

"Face the fact that Dad isn't coming back."

Silence. Then Mom forces a smile, and there's a hint of fondness in it. She always thinks about the happy times first. But the smile dies, and her features darken—it never fails to come after. Reliving the moments she's done everything to forget. "You've never asked about your father before. I kept waiting for it to happen, but you never did." Her gaze meets mine.

I remember pieces of him. An image of stained workboots by the door, the rumble of a man's voice above me. I know that his name was Luke, and he was good at whistling. And when I picture him leaving us, walking out that door for the last time, he's whistling so loudly that he can't hear Mom begging him to stay. The rest of it doesn't matter, really. It never did. "I knew it would hurt you," is all I say.

Mom nods, pursing her lips. "So what's changed?"

"Me," I answer simply. When she doesn't say anything, I stoop to kiss her cheek. "If you can't do it for yourself, do this for us, okay? Pack everything into boxes, and give it to Nick. Or throw it out in the snow, it doesn't matter. Just move on. Call Hubert Gill and go on a date. Finish one of your stories and send it out into the world."

She gives me another pained smile. There's a brightness

in her eyes now, the sheen of tears, and I hate that I've put it there. "You always dreamed bigger than the rest of us, Ivy," she says.

As an answer, I rest my head on her shoulder and close my eyes, wishing those dreams would stay far, far away.

• • •

Seven hours later, Mom wakes up on her own again.

Seven hours later, Lorna emerges from her room and eats breakfast at the kitchen table.

Seven hours later, I start getting ready for my last day of school.

Mom sings in the shower at the top of her lungs. I listen in the hallway for just a moment, smiling to myself. Somehow, I did it. Everything is falling into place, my place. I move into the living room. I spot my bag by Spencer Hille's cage, right beside Lorna's foot. "I'll see you later," I say to her as I approach.

"Going to that nursing home again?" Lorna asks. She's holding a yellow legal pad, and there's a pen in her hand. She chews on the end of it. A bowl of soggy cereal is untouched by her elbow.

"School, actually. We have dress rehearsal in a half hour. Tomorrow is opening night, and Chuck wants to make sure we're ready. Remember what I taught you," I mutter to our parrot as I bend over.

"What are you saying to him?" Lorna asks. She scribbles a line across the page.

I shoulder my bag, straight-faced. "I thought I would

teach him something else. We've been working on it the past week or so."

Her head jerks up, and her green eyes are narrow. "You taught my baby something? Like what? Ivy, what did you teach him? *Ivy.* Damn it, Ivy, *what did you teach him?*" my sister shouts at my back.

"There's more to life than being beautiful, dear sister."

"Ivy taught the parrot something new?" Unnoticed, Mom has come out of the bathroom and stands in the hall, hair dripping, towel falling from the sloppy knot by her armpit. I wave at her and make a beeline for the door.

Livid, Lorna opens her mouth to demand an answer from me again. But then Spencer Hille squawks, "You're a strong, independent woman!"

Mom bursts out laughing.

Chapter Thirty-Three

The cold pulls me away from dreamland.

Disoriented, it takes me a moment to realize where I am—this is not my room or the trailer park. An old building squats in a field, surrounded by the remains of a chain link fence. It must be the middle of the night, since the sky is at its blackest. Not even the moon wants to be here. Shivering, I turn around. The feeble light at the top of the pole reveals the tracks, and the lined-up train cars. The depot. Of course, it's Friday night. The canvas waits for me, a giant, metal beast.

I automatically shuffle toward the office to retrieve my spray paint. My sweatpants flatten against my thighs in the wind. Thankfully, I went to bed wearing a hoodie, and I've taken to putting on thick socks before falling asleep. With the cans pressed to my chest, I step over the first set of tracks and stop in front of the closest car, frowning. This one is round and rusted. There's a gang symbol exploding over the surface in violent hues of green and orange. It's too big to cover or work around, so I pick my way farther down the lineup.

There—one of the cars is nearly untouched. It's square and flat and beckons to me with its potential.

I stand in front of it for what feels like hours. I know I don't have much longer to do something. But for some reason, I can't. My sleepy brain keeps thinking, *Tonight. It all ends tonight.* Vanessa's face stares back from the insides of my eyelids. It's not Myers, Miranda, or anyone in my family.

Suddenly I know why I've been walking in my sleep. Looking for Vanessa night after night. Waking up outside her bedroom window. Something that Amar said one night at the diner helps me realize it, the thing about the elephants. Then Chuck's voice sounds in my head, saying, *This is a story of resolutions, farewells, tying up loose ends. It's about the power of one person to change what she can in the little time she has left.*

Vanessa and I never had our farewells.

This will be my last time at the depot. I know that. Someone else in my situation might spray something complex, intricate, utterly memorable. An image worthy of final moments. But me? I can only leave what I have left.

Just a few minutes later I step back and look up at it. A thousand emotions and memories fight and collide inside me. In the middle of it all...her.

Maybe if enough people see the words, maybe if the words travel through enough places, maybe if they're given enough time, she'll see them. Somewhere. Someday. Somehow. All that matters is that they're no longer trapped inside of me. This is my contribution to that locker at school.

Goodbye, Vanessa.

• • •

The weather warning is issued for midnight.

I spend my last Saturday as I always do. I start at the lumberyard, watching Myers from behind the tree. Next I go to Hallett to visit the usual residents for the last time; Russell is asleep, but Eunice is alert and eager to lament the universe. After that, it's the final dress rehearsal. The hour passes in a blur, I say goodbye over and over until it almost feels meaningless.

Afterward, Chuck just sits in his seat and looks at us. He doesn't smile, he doesn't laugh, he doesn't cry. He just says, "Like that. Do it exactly like that tonight." His eyes meet mine. I'm the first one to turn away.

Ignoring the intensity of Mitch's frown and Amanda's stare, I leave the auditorium and rush to my car. By the time the heat melts the frost on the windshield and I get home, it's after six. There's just one hour left until I have to be back at the school and put on my costume.

Only five hours, twenty-two minutes, and fifty-one seconds left on my timer.

Mom and Lorna are crowded in the bathroom, fighting for the curling iron. The stereo is blaring. "Are you ready?" I ask tightly, watching them. My stomach is writhing. Any semblance of acceptance I've managed to find over the past few days is fast diminishing.

My sister seizes the iron with a triumphant sound. Mom rolls her eyes and shoves past. A trail of perfume follows as she enters her disastrous room. "Just a second," she mutters. "Let me find my earrings." I hover nearby, noting that Dad's things are scattered. Some of it has been put in boxes—she's really doing it.

A framed picture catches my eye where it rests on a stack of folded T-shirts. Frowning, I pick it up.

A pearl gleams in Mom's left earlobe as she turns and notices the movement. "What are you looking at?" she asks, angling her head to fasten the other earring. It's been a long time since she's done her hair like that, all wild and free.

"I've never seen this one." I hold it up for a moment before looking at the three faces again. Two young children, obviously Mom and Uncle Nick. A middle-aged woman with a bad perm and big glasses has her arms around them. Her hair is cringeworthy red and they're all in front of a fireplace made of orange bricks. I'm strangely drawn to the image.

Mom spares it a cursory glance. Distaste flits across her face. "Oh, I've been packing up some stuff." She yanks a pair of pantyhose out of her top dresser drawer. She hops as she puts them on. "I found that in a pile today." She shimmies the pantyhose the rest of the way up and adjusts the skirt of her green dress. Her breasts jiggle; the neckline is a deep *V.* If Hubert Gill sees her tonight, he's going to have a heart attack.

"Who is that?" I ask her, pointing to the woman. Lorna makes a frustrated noise in the bathroom and there's a clatter, probably the curling iron falling to the floor.

We both ignore her. Mom hurries back to the closet

and kneels. "That's your grandmother," she answers breath-lessly. "On my side. Neither of you met her since she died just after Lorna was born. I didn't want her anywhere near my family anyway—that woman used to beat the crap out of Nick."

Mindless of the way my frown deepens, Mom throws a bunch of shoes aside. She leans back, heels in hand, and shoves her feet in them. She then stands, pulls her nice coat off the hanger, and shrugs it on. "We're all driving together, right?" she tosses over her shoulder.

I barely hear her. I'm staring at the picture so hard that my eyes begin to strain.

Comprehension slams into me like a freight train. "Oh, my God," I whisper. The picture falls from my sudden-ly-limp fingers. The glass cracks and scatters on the carpet.

Swearing, Mom rushes to my side. Lorna appears in the doorway, with just one of her eyes darkened with mascara. She looks from me to the picture and her brow furrows. "What? What is it?" Mom steps over the broken frame and tugs at my arm, away from the mess.

My mind is spinning. I pull free of Mom's grip. "N-nothing. I just saw the clock. Come on, we're late." I swallow. Lick my dry lips. Pretend I can't feel their stares boring into my back as I go down the hall and toward the front door. I'm a robot, a machine and nothing more. There are no thoughts, no feelings besides this dull throb-bing in my head. But when Mom and Lorna catch up with me, both still frowning, a single thought breaks through. A senseless, endless chant. *It can't be, it can't be, it can't be.*

We go outside. It's dark and the cold wraps its icy body around mine, freezing my damp eyelashes and hair. We all pile into Mom's car. Me in the front, Lorna in the back. Denial is a bitter taste in my mouth. It can't be. It just can't.

The silence doesn't last long after the car jolts into motion. "I know it's scary, going up there in front of everyone," Mom says soothingly. "But you're going to do great. We'll be in the front row, cheering you on. Just like Susie promised." Snow beats against the windshield, and the wipers are frantic in their back-and-forth motion.

Suddenly I come alive. I claw at the door, shouting, "Wait, wait!" It's locked. With frantic fingers I shove at the button. *Click.* We're just passing Mrs. Jones's place when I open the door and look down at the moving ground. Idiot is going wild.

"Jesus, Ivy!" Mom slams on the brakes, and they squeal as the car shudders to a halt.

A song on the radio plays, filling the shocked silence. Something sad and country. "I have to take my own car," I tell Mom around the lump in my throat. "Sorry. I forgot."

Both of them are staring at me with wide eyes. The door is still open on my side, and wind whistles through the narrow space. Snowflakes get caught on the upholstery. "Are you okay?" Mom asks after a long, long pause.

I think I nod and mumble some appropriate response. *Fine. Just fine. See you there.* Gripping the top of the car for support, I stand on shaky feet. Slam the door shut. I walk away, still feeling their unbroken stares. *Nerves*, they'll probably tell themselves. They have no idea that my heart is breaking.

Because I know who the killer is.

Chapter Thirty-Four

The lights are blinding. They shine down on me, making my skin a flawless, glowing white. As if I'm already dead.

Mitch Donovan and I stand facing each other, so close I could reach up and touch the tear that hovers on the edge of his jaw. All of Kennedy watches us, and the weight of their stares is nothing compared to the way Mitch is looking at me.

"We both did horrible things to each other," I tell him tremulously. Someone in the audience coughs. "We were both stupid and stubborn. But I care about you, and I won't give up." With my eyes I will him to hear the words unspoken: *I didn't mean to hurt Vanessa. I always planned to be with her that last night. I wasn't the one who took her from us.*

A muscle juts in Mitch's jaw, and he looks as if he doesn't know whether to lash out or listen to what I'm saying. We have so much history. He teased Vanessa and me endlessly as children, chasing, poking, playing, taunting. He reminded Vanessa to take her shots and he ruffled my hair when he walked by. He used to smile.

"...don't know how to forgive you," Mitch recites. Maybe he's thinking about our pasts, too, because the line is all razor edges and venom.

"Just try. That's all I ask." My voice is soft, yet it carries through the empty space of the auditorium and echoes. *All I ask...all I ask...all I ask...*

As the script dictates, Mitch brushes a curl off my brow. His skin is hot and his voice husky. "For you...or for me?" he asks. He lowers his hand quickly, and it fists at his side.

"Both, maybe."

Five seconds tick by. Everyone waits. Finally, Mitch says, "I think I was wrong. About everything."

That line isn't in the script.

With those unexpected words, it's over. The scene, the play, the night. I don't have a chance to reply. Blinking rapidly, Mitch walks off the opposite end of the stage. I stand there for a few moments, looking after him. Then, slowly, I turn around too. My steps are measured, and I stop and sway as if I'm dizzy. I put a hand to my forehead. Joan Picks appears on the stage, a tiny girl who's on the squad and also Shannon's best friend—the narrator.

"It happened on a Wednesday," she tells the silent crowd. "Emily lies in bed, her face turned towards the sun. She thinks of lost love and friendships lost and everything gained. And she dies."

I'm hidden behind the curtain when she utters that final line. It strikes a chord within me, and I falter again. It's the simplicity of the words, the pitiless truth. *And she dies.*

There's no time to drown in self-pity; some of my classmates come up and clap me on the shoulder. There are *good jobs* and *that was great* and *I almost cried* from all around. Chuck towers above us, and his beard splits with a rare smile. "You were amazing, Ivy," he says. "I knew you could do it."

"I seriously felt like you and Mitch were about to make out or kill each other," Chris Moody, Bill Moody's younger brother, comments. "What was going through your head?"

Before I can answer, applause and cheering disrupts the stillness—it's time to go back out there and take our bows. Some of the other kids begin to trickle away, and I follow them to the brilliance of the stage. Hand in hand, the entire drama class stretches across the platform. Being my co-lead, Mitch has no choice but to stand beside me. This time his grip isn't so tight and hot. Instead, it's gentle. Looser. Like he's ready to let go.

I search the faces in the seats. As promised, there's Mom, Lorna, Uncle Nick, Amar, and Susie in the front row. They all have pride in their expressions. Yet another lump forms in my throat when Uncle Nick puts two fingers to his mouth and whistles for me. Too soon, we're all returning to obscurity behind the curtains. Everyone immediately scatters to find their families or take off costumes. Yards away, Amanda pushes Shannon to the side, completely ignoring the cheerleader's loud complaint. She spots me. She looks pretty, with her dreads tied back in a bun and makeup highlighting her eyes and cheeks. "Hey, your mom is looking for you," Amanda calls. Flapping my hand in acknowledgment, I start to walk away, but her raised voice stops me again. "I know what you did, by the way."

I pause. "What do you mean?"

Amanda reaches me, out of breath. She glares at Joan as she passes, then focuses on my face again. "I'm being transferred," she replies. "To a different home. Apparently some complaints were made about old lady Biscoe. Rachel Donovan has been getting foster home certification, I guess, and since she'll have an opening soon it looks like I'll be going there."

Rachel Donovan? Really? It's strange to think of that family taking someone in—Amanda is as different from Vanessa as tears are to laughter—but then I think of Rachel standing in that frozen food aisle by herself, and I see her hovering over a grave. Maybe this is good for everyone. "That's great," I say, trying to sound enthusiastic.

A combination of amusement and annoyance glints in Amanda's gaze. "Are you always such a busybody?" she demands.

"I don't know what you're talking about."

My almost-friend rolls her eyes. "Yeah, yeah. But I appreciate it. Really."

I head for the stairs, forcing a grin at her over my shoulder. "If I find out who helped you, I'll pass it along."

"See you Monday?" she shouts after me, choosing to ignore this.

The question makes me hesitate where I shouldn't; there won't be any more days. Just hours, and those are swiftly counting down. "Definitely. Monday," I manage. My voice is strange, even to my own ears. Strangled. Amanda's eyes narrow, and I get the sense that she perceives more than anyone else. She might even suspect the truth, or at least part of it. Quickly, I turn my back on her and descend the stairs. And that's the last time I'll ever see Amanda Ryan, the strange girl who cuts and tempts fate and notices.

I go in search of my family. But just as I pass through the auditorium doors and into the cafeteria, someone puts a hand on my arm. I turn to face Brent. Feeling self-conscious in my Emily costume, which is a pink dress that stops just above the knees, I glance over my shoulder in hopes of spotting Mom or Lorna. "Look, I need to talk to—" I start.

"I just wanted to let you know that you were great," he interrupts. A laugh erupts behind us, and conversations bounce off the dome ceiling.

"Thanks, Brent."

"Also, I told Allen about what happened on the night of the winter formal. Mitch didn't even deny it when the deputies confronted him. So it's up to you, if you want to press charges."

At this, I blink. If Mitch admitted that what he did that night was wrong, maybe what happened onstage wasn't just my imagination—maybe we really have reached some kind of resolution between us.

Brent is still waiting for me to respond, so I mumble, "Uh, I'll think about it." It occurs to me that this is the last time I'll ever talk to him, too. But I don't know what to say, so I turn away. I make it a couple feet when he speaks.

"He still loves you, you know."

My heart stumbles—there's no mistaking who Brent means. I turn, gluing my attention to the floor. I don't want to talk about this, I can't talk about this. "Love fades," I reply flatly.

There's a pause. Brent lowers his voice. "Why would

you want it to?" A genuinely puzzled note rings in the words, and pain shines from his eyes.

"Maybe this is the way things are meant to be." I shrug and try to convince both of us that I'm content with it.

"I've never believed in fate," he counters.

"No?" It's all I believe in. The numbers never lie.

Now Brent sighs. "No. Which is why I've been such an idiot these past few months. You might be attracted to me, but you don't look at me the way you look at him. Not even close. That's how I know we make our own choices. You've always chosen him." Brent says this without self-pity, without bitterness. The way someone would tell an absolute truth.

Someone shoulders past me. "I-I'm sorry," I stammer, glancing over my shoulder.

When I turn back, I see that Brent hasn't taken his gaze off me. "Don't be," he says. "Just don't break his heart again. He doesn't deserve it."

Of all people, of all conversations, I wasn't expecting this from him, here and now. It's obvious that he's picturing Vanessa with these words; he'll never have a second chance with her.

Myers. My heart aches when I realize the night of the dance will be my last memory of him. Can I really leave it like that? Should I? He no longer belongs to me. And when I'm gone, maybe Ginger will be the one to put that broken heart back together.

The noise around me heightens as I think, remembering everything, aware this is a choice that will define me. The words and memories blend together, all of them but one—Myers. And I know, just as certainly as he knew he was in love with me, that I can't leave this world without seeing him one more time. I won't allow history to repeat itself and let my last night be like Vanessa's. I want more than eight seconds. "I have to go," I say.

"Ivy—"

"Find my family," I say. It's seized me now, the desperate desire to get to Myers. "Tell them…tell them not to wait up. And that I love them. Will you do that?" My voice quavers.

Just like Amanda, Brent hears something in my voice. Simply, he says, "Okay."

But I don't go, not yet. I smile again, a wobbly thing. "I wish I hadn't wasted so much time being mad," I say. "Thanks, Brent. For everything. It was my fault, what happened that night we kissed. I just want you to know that."

For once, I've rendered him speechless. His expression is the same one he wore when we were standing outside the diner, by the dumpsters. This time I recognize it—resignation. I know now that Brent had his own reasons for kissing me back during the party, reasons that had nothing to do with alcohol or numbers.

Without giving him a chance to recover, I find the exit. No time to change or get my coat. I stare at the numbers above me as I open the door, watch their blinding reflection in the glass. Snowflakes swirl beyond them. Night beckons. The storm is coming.

Two hours left.

• • •

A frenzy has gripped my bones and it won't let go. As I drive to his house it feels as if I'm lifting out of my body. Everything is fuzzy and hazed, sharp and painful all at once. Like I'm a live wire. There's not enough time and I'm not ready. To say goodbye to Myers, to face the killer, to accept my end. Any of it.

His driveway appears. I stare at the mailbox, and the name on it glints. PATRIPSKI. In my quivering vision the letters get bigger, then shrink down. My breathing is uneven as I guide the car down the narrow road and park in front of the garage. The lights are on; he's home. This is it.

I can't do this. I even shift gears to reverse and leave this place behind. Why do I need to endure every small pain, face every fear before the end? Isn't it enough, the torture of knowing?

His voice whispers through my mind. *You gave up on me.*

Damn it.

Before I can talk myself out of it, I cut the engine and step into the cold. The air marks my rapid breathing during my trek. There are no cars, and I know the Patripskis rarely park in the garage—it probably means no one is home yet. My heart sinks. What if I don't get to see him?

Without letting myself reconsider, I knock on the door. The sound echoes, but there's no response. I cry out, slamming the wood with the side of my fist, as if that will make him appear.

"Ivy?"

Myers is coming up the walkway. He looks so good that it hurts. Jeans hug his hips, his torso is long and lean, his strong jawline is clean of stubble. I want him, here and now.

As if Myers hears my thoughts, our eyes meet and he goes still. "I looked for you after the play," he says. He doesn't seem surprised that I'm here, and somehow I'm not surprised that he was there. There's an invisible string between the two of us, connecting and tugging. For a moment we don't speak.

After two quick steps, we collide in heat made of want and desperation. His hands slide around my waist and jerk me so close I can feel every part of him against me. I taste him one last time, memorizing it, adoring it, wishing it would never stop. My arms are too tight around his neck, but he doesn't utter a single complaint. He pulls away for just an instant to kiss my eyelids, my cheek, and then he's back on my mouth. My heart chants his name. *Myers. Myers. Myers.*

Somehow I manage to step away. My lips feel swollen, and I welcome the way they tingle.

He lets me go. His expression is strained, as if he wants to say something. He hasn't accepted that there is nothing to say, so I give him a smile that makes the words unnecessary. It conveys how much I love him, how much I regret and how much I'll miss. This was all I wanted—just one more moment. "Bye, Myers," I say softly. I start to walk past him.

"Ivy."

I stop and face him again. He's frowning. If I let myself linger another second, I'll break. "See you around, okay?" I say, walking backward and waving. When Myers doesn't respond—he's still staring at me, like he's seen something for the first time—I force myself to get in my car and slam the door shut. It's not enough, because even with glass and metal between us I can feel the pull of him. It's a magnetic force I've never been able to resist.

There are tears in my eyes as I turn the key in the ignition. The engine roars to life, and he's still standing where I left him. He doesn't move.

The moment I reach the road, I accelerate. Distance doesn't ease the anguish; I know I'll never see Myers Patripski again.

I drive through the night and feeling rises within me. Higher, hotter. At the last second, I swerve violently to the right, jump out, run into the ditch, and vomit in the snow. A sour taste explodes in my mouth. Shuddering, I wipe my lips clean with the back of my sleeve. It's unavoidable—I'm scared. I'm so scared I can't think straight.

The crisp air and bare branches of the trees harden my resolve again. Snow glistens, and a savage wind warns of the storm that's coming. It makes me think of that night in Havenger's. Except that after tonight, there won't be any more deaths. I lean my palms on my knees and focus on breathing. Inhale. Exhale. An hour and a half left. I can do this. I can.

It's time.

Chapter Thirty-Five

I put a note in the killer's mailbox, a simple piece of paper with the same words that lured Vanessa out into the night nearly five months ago.

Meet me in Havenger's.

To make sure it isn't missed, I put up the flag. I don't leave right away, thought. I stand next to the mailbox and look at the house. Every window is dark. There are no tracks in the driveway, no footprints in the snow—he hasn't been here yet. But he'll come. Soon.

And I keep thinking, *I should have known.*

A few minutes later I peel myself away, get back into my car, and drive to Havenger's.

It takes fifteen minutes. I park on the side of the road. The slam of the car door resonates through the frosty air. There's an extra coat, scarf, and boots in my back seat for emergencies. Perfect for tonight's storm. It's approaching fast now, pushing violently against my car, blinding Kennedy with all the white.

I put on the coat. It's old and too tight across the shoulders. The boots are too small, also. I wrap the scarf around my neck, the only thing that really fits. It's strange, thinking that these clothes are what they're going to find me in. If I'm ever found, that is. The wind howls as I stand there and gaze up at the stars fighting to shine through wisps of clouds, thinking of astronomy class, of all things. *Some go quietly, some end their lives in an explosion of brilliance.* I wonder how Vanessa went.

No, I don't wonder. I know. Vanessa would have fought, and fought hard.

The thought of her urges me on. Dipping into the ditch and up the small hill, I head for that place, the patch of woods where I found her body. Vanessa and I once shared everything. It seems only fitting we should share this, too.

As I push through the cold, I take a disposable phone from the pocket of Emily's dress. I'd bought it at the general store earlier, after separating from Mom and Lorna, and there's only one number programmed into the contact list. I press talk with my thumb and hold the phone to my ear; already it feels like a box of ice.

It rings once. Twice. Three times. Four times. Then it goes to voicemail. My heart pounds harder and faster. I quickly hit the TALK button again. I'm so anxious that I stop where I am and lean against a tree, shivering. Visible swirls in the air mark each breath. If he doesn't answer, this entire thing will be for nothing. The note, coming out here, my death. I grit my teeth, silently willing him to pick up. Pick up, pick up, pick up!

Then, suddenly, he does. "Hello?" He sounds groggy.

I almost cry with relief. "Allen, it's Ivy."

There's an instant change to his voice. Exasperated, dismissive. Ever since the Crookston girl disappeared, his temper has been worse than usual. "Ivy, I don't have time for—"

"I need you to listen to me. If you have a way to record this conversation, do it." I start walking again. He begins to argue, of course. I talk over him. "I'm in Havenger's Woods. I have a half hour left, I think. The man who killed all those girls is coming for me."

Allen stops. "How—"

"Search his house. You'll probably find the evidence you need in the basement." And then I give him the name.

For the first time, Allen McCork takes me seriously. There's real alarm in his tone now. "Damn it, Ivy—"

"I'm putting the phone in my pocket now. I'll get a full confession out of him, I promise. Good luck, Allen." Over his protests, I tuck it into a hiding place against my heart. I don't let myself worry about whether or not the signal will remain steady.

My scarf flutters in the wind. My glasses fog as I put my hand out. When a snowflake settles onto my skin, the chill lasts only an instant before the little thing dissolves. I tilt my chin up, and the black sky dances with millions and millions of drifting pieces. The beauty of it is lost on me. Here, alone, with a moment to comprehend everything, I've never known such pain and betrayal. How could I have missed it?

As an answer, Russell's gruff voice sounds in my head, *Usually the answers we're looking for are right in front of us. And sometimes…we see what we want to see.*

For some reason, as I wait there in the cold, I remember summer. The shimmering heat waves, the flashing and fading of fireflies in the grass, the sugary sweetness of roasted marshmallows over a fire. I recall the slow progress of sweat down my spine, the sound of water lapping the shore of the lake, the unison of voices during a children's game of hopscotch.

I would have liked to see summer again.

Snap.

Even though I've been expecting it, the sound startles me. Terror turns the moisture in my mouth to chalk. Slowly, I turn to face him. The physical form of all my nightmares during these past five months. The man who murdered Vanessa and the other girls. The man who will take my life, as well. He stands in a shaft of sudden moonlight, watching me with sadness in his blue eyes. My eyes.

I smile bitterly. "Hi, Uncle Nick."

Chapter Thirty-Six

His voice is so cold, it sends a shard of ice through my heart. As if he's a stranger.

"It didn't have to be this way," he tells me.

It feels as if everything has stopped. The snow, the seconds, the planet. There's too much to say, and it all crowds in my throat and renders me utterly incapable of speech.

Uncle Nick stands just a few feet away. The approaching storm has hidden the moonlight, but a flashlight in his hand illuminates the area around us. It allows me to note the way his fingers are twitching again. For the first time, it occurs to me that it isn't a habit born from a need for cigarettes, but from another need entirely. The thought is just one more knife to my heart.

When I still don't respond, my uncle adds, "How did you know it was me? Did you see my face, that night in the woods? During the formal?"

The question jars me. I swallow and answer, "No. Mom showed me a picture of your family. There was a vase of gardenias behind your mother, on the mantle. That's when I knew."

It had been a shot in the dark—just a gut feeling, really—but something in his eyes flickers. I've surprised him. He shakes his head. "God, we hated that woman." It's eerie now, how alike he and Mom sound: she'd said the exact same thing. Uncle Nick lets out a breath. "Even from the grave she's screwing with me."

Now I know for sure. Salt explodes in my mouth from the tears streaking down my face. This man is so familiar, so dear. He's not wearing a coat, even with a storm coming. That same old sweater keeps him warm, as it always has. It used to keep me warm when I sat on his lap, during Christmases and football games. He's still thinking about his mother, I can tell from his furrowed brow.

I finally ask the one question that has been haunting me for months. Every second of every day. "*Why?*" The syllable echoes through the trees.

If I expected him to look ashamed, I'm met with disappointment. My uncle just looks thoughtful, as if he's unsure how to begin. He shifts from foot to foot. "My…hobby is a hunger. No, think of it like an itch. I need to scratch it every once in a while," he says. Somewhere else, saying anything else, he could be talking about the weather.

"But why *Vanessa*?" I cry, clenching my fists. I want to hate him so badly, and part of me does.

Uncle Nick doesn't react. He continues to watch me in that detached, predatory way. He's considering how much time we have left before the storm hits. Maybe contemplating ending this right now. Panic bubbles up; Allen doesn't have enough yet. "Answer me, damn it! You *owe* me this!" It ends in a scream.

After another beat of hesitation, Uncle Nick shrugs. Like the decision was so inconsequential. Goosebumps rises on my skin. "I saw the way she treated you," he replies. His gaze darkens. "Like she was better. It made the choice easy."

"But—"

"Everything about that night should have gone differently," he goes on in a murmur. It seems like he's talking to himself. "You shouldn't have gotten to her house before me. I never meant for anyone to see the note and the flower. And you shouldn't have found her in Havenger's. God, none of this would be happening if that night had gone according to plan."

There's real regret in the way he says it—he's not the stranger anymore, the monster. I don't know if that makes this better or worse. "What about Jill? Was she part of a plan?" I ask faintly, trying not to be sick again. "What about the girl from Crookston?"

He takes a step closer. "The girl at the diner was an impulse. I saw her, and I wanted her. It didn't take long. I was back in my office before anyone knew I was gone. It was the same with the one from Crookston. But the first body was a problem, and that's why I came out here on the night of your winter formal. I was going to try to bury it. Then you messed everything up again, by being there and seeing me. I didn't know what to do." Another step.

"There's more I need to know," I blurt, stalling. He halts and tilts his head in question. I force the words out. "Why did the florist have Myers's name on the gardenia order? And why did you put the gloves in Mitch's room?"

Irritation flashes across his expression. "Because those kids are trash, Ivy," Uncle Nick growls. There's the protective man I've always known. "I stole his card one night at the diner. Then I paid someone to go into the florist's, pick the flowers up for me, and sign the receipt with Patripski's name. I figured if McCork ever did track the flower down, he would prosecute him. The boy deserved it, especially after what he did to you. Same with Donovan and the gloves. As an added bonus, they would throw you off my trail. Except none of it worked."

Instantly a defense for Myers rises to my lips. I hold it back when I see that Uncle Nick has taken two more steps. "You're going to kill me now, aren't you?" I breathe. But it doesn't come out as a question. All the instincts that shriek *survival* have gone quiet, and something inside me settles into a sensation like resignation. Yet, even though time proves there is no fighting it, I won't die like some pitiful excuse for a star. A memory slams into me, an image of Russell's room and a poetry book in my hands. *Do not go gentle into that good night...rage, rage against the dying of the light.*

Uncle Nick stands right in front of me, hands shoved in his pockets, smiling forlornly at the ground. Seeing something that I don't. "I was there when you were born, did you know that?" he asks fondly. "I hated doing this to you. Following you to the Halloween party, leaving the note and the gardenia, hurting you in the auditorium. You're too smart, though. Way smarter than that idiot Allen McCork. I always knew that if you tried, you would find me. So I did everything I could to scare you away. *Why didn't you stop looking?*"

Only once, in my entire life, have I heard my uncle raise his voice. It's horrible. Awful. Terrifying. It takes me a few tries, but eventually I manage to whisper, "Because everyone else already had."

A sound leaves his throat, something between a laugh and a sigh. "Ivy. Always so different. I meant what I said in my office, kid. I love you."

With those words, something clicks into place. And I know. I'm finally ready. "I love you, too," I whisper, tensing.

He lunges for me.

I dive out of the way. He checks himself, but it's too late; I'm scrambling to my feet and weaving through the trees. My hands are numb and my blood has turned to terror in my veins. He's following me. I can hear twigs breaking beneath his weight. He's close, too close. Sobbing, I raise my gaze. Through spaces between the branches, I see the lake. There are only more trees beyond it, but I pump my arms harder. Run faster. My instincts are drawn to that dark plateau of ice.

Without warning, a fierce hand tangles in my hair and wrenches my head back—just like that night in the auditorium—and I scream, twisting away. He doesn't let go, but before he can do anything more I lash out with my booted foot. It collides with something hard. Uncle Nick shouts and suddenly I'm free. I bolt again. He screams my name.

The lake opens up before me, wide and dark and still. Struggling to maintain my balance on the ice, I spin to face Uncle Nick, gasping for air. My lungs burn. He emerges from the shadows, a bloody scratch along one of his cheeks. "It's no use, Ivy!" he pants, bending to catch his breath. "You don't have anywhere to run."

I keep backing away, watching the numbers over his head. Only five minutes left. He stalks me, his eyes so lifeless and cold that dying suddenly isn't the worst prospect—becoming someone like him is. Near the middle of the lake, I stop. He does, too, evaluating me. Trying to guess my next move. "I'm not going anywhere, Uncle Nick," I say brokenly. And I take one more step back.

Crack.

The ground beneath our feet shudders. Uncle Nick's eyes widen as he realizes the danger. I smile through my tears. *Goodbye.*

And we both fall.

Cold. Freezing. Numb. Needles. Agony. The water closes in around me, a shimmering blue-black that's deceptive in its beauty. It rushes into my mouth, my ears, my lungs. The pain is instant and agonizing. I try to scream, but a stream of bubbles is all that emerges.

Somehow I manage to move my arms and legs. My hand strikes something hard, and I flatten my palm against it. Ice, slick to the touch. I follow it to where I think I fell through, but don't find the opening. Already my head is becoming light, prickling. Air. I need air. Instinct urges me on; I have to keep going. I use the ice as a guide and kick my way forward. Everything becomes darkness. Hysteria claws up my throat, threatening to burst from me in a scream that would result in swallowing more water and effectively eliminate what little air I have left. For an instant I wonder where Uncle Nick is. But then I remember his timer, and I know he can never hurt anyone again. He's here somewhere with me. Losing air, too. Losing sensation, too.

Dying, too.

My coat hinders me. My movements are slow as I pull it off, let it float away into oblivion. It doesn't help much. My bones have become some thick metal. It's hard, so hard to cut through the icy depths.

I wave my arms, frantic to reach the surface. But wherever I am, I've become lost in the deep. There's no bottom and no surface now. Just lovely, wet death, waiting to take me. Still I struggle. My hair clouds in front of my eyes, and I try to shove it away, though there's nothing to see. Pain rips through me, and suddenly I know.

This is it. This is my end.

Then none of it seems important. Decades pass in the icy obscurity. I lose sense of which way is up and which way is down. I try to *think*, but all I can see are images. My mom's fingers on the keys. Vanessa's bright smile. Myers's soft eyes.

Pressure builds in my lungs, and eventually I stop. Stop everything. I can't go any farther. The lake is a merciless foe. I have fought and I have lost. No, I've won. I've won. The people I care about are safe now, they have a chance to be happy. My eyes flutter shut, and my insides scream. I hold on, somehow. I don't inhale the ink surrounding me. Not yet. My head pounds and prickles. And suddenly, even if I can't see them, I can *feel* the numbers.

Nine. Eight. Seven.

The end looms closer. After so much pain and toil, it's almost a relief. I drift, and finally, finally, I give up. The water is swift and eager and greedy. It rushes in. Any warmth that was left ebbs away. The frozen darkness wants me—its arms are tight and numbing. I remember hearing about how the heart beats one hundred thousand times in one day, but I can hear mine and I know that it's no longer true.

Six. Five. Four.

Black clouds drift across my vision. They merge and became a storm of quiet pain.

Three.

My insides go still as the water fills every vein. Slowly my arms spread, as if I'm about to take flight.

Two.

Death reaches for me in the dark.

One.

And I soar into its embrace.

Chapter Thirty-Seven

"You're not leaving me."

Down. Down. Down.

Everything is dark. Numb. Disorienting. There are hands on my chest, pushing so hard that my bones are close to breaking. My eyes open. I see only splotches of black and white. My nostrils flare, absorbing the scent of night. Something is bent over my prone form. A shadow. It doesn't stop pushing, and slowly I regain more of my senses—it's trying to bring me back. The pain is unbearable. I fight the return, clinging to the darkness.

"You have to stay. Please, Ivy. For me."

A distant part of my mind recognizes the voice now; I would know it anywhere. But the name...the name escapes me...

Then I feel warms lips pressing fiercely against mine, air forces its way inside. It leaves a moment later, rejected. The black splotches grow. Rough hands suddenly smack my cheeks. "Damn it, Ivy!" They shake me so hard my teeth rattle. Those lips crush mine again. More air.

I shoot upright and spew water everywhere.

The shadow wraps an arm around me to make sure I don't fall back. I wheeze and sway, the gray world tilting. My head lolls in the crook of an elbow and everything is so vibrant and burning. "I know it hurts, and it would be easier to let go," the voice growls. The arms tighten. "But if you need a reason to keep fighting, know that I love you. That should be enough."

Like a comet through the velvet expanse of sky, his name comes to me. This has to be another taunting illusion, more desperate whispers from the corners of my mind.

"Myers?" I say it with every feeling I possess, painting his name with dripping sorrow, drying pain, some cracked emotion that resembles hope. I can't find him with my eyes, but I know he's gazing down at my face. He's always seen me, somehow, which is something that can't be said of any other being on this fast-tilting planet. I shove the words past the choking sensation of death, and it seems fitting that they might be my last: "Thanks for the dance."

If he replies, I don't hear it. The last thing I ever see is the dozens and dozens of stars—they can't be real, since the storm is on us—and they seem to be speaking. Millions of fragile whispers that consume my senses. *I'm here. I'm here. I'm here.*

But I'm not.

Chapter Thirty-Eight

In heaven, there's a painting of a duck.

I didn't expect that. I didn't expect heaven to have walls, actually, or a TV that blares into the stillness. I didn't expect it to hurt so much, either. Moaning quietly, I lift my hand to touch something. Anything. But it's too hard, so I concentrate on seeing instead. Soft edges harden into reality.

There's movement out of the corner of my eye. My head swivels to the right. I don't know what I think I'll find—an angel?—but my mother asleep in a chair isn't it. She's in the rumpled clothes she wore to the play, and drool leaks out of her mouth.

I start to wake her, to ask her what's happening, but a hum in my ears becomes a voice. I search for it and realize it's coming from a woman on the screen. She stares at me from behind the glass, clutching a thick microphone. In the background I see Uncle Nick's house. My heart skips a beat. "…one will be able to forget the day they searched

Nick Erickson's house and discovered the body of Jill Briggs in the basement," she's saying. She adds something about gardenias that I don't catch. "…one will ever forget the day the sheriff and his deputies searched Havenger's Woods and found seven other girls buried under the frozen dirt."

And then she lists them. One by one. Their names are forever imprinted on my soul. Alyssa Song, Lane Hutchinson, Molly Foster, Bree Macheska, Peyton Norton, Ellie Red. A dancer, a young mother, a nursing student, a tattoo artist, a singer, a basketball player. Because of Nick Erickson, they will never be more.

Then Kailey Bray's faces flashes onto the screen.

"Mom?" I finally croak, devastated. She doesn't move. I want the TV *off*. "Mom?"

She sits up a little, then slumps back down. She grips the armrests of the chair so tightly the wood creaks. "You're awake." Releasing the armrests, she rubs her eyes, as if she's dreamed of this before and doesn't believe it now. Something is different about her, but I can't put my finger on it—my thoughts are too fuzzy. When Mom looks at me again and I stare back at her, she crumples. Sobs wrench through her, violent, gulping heaves. Helpless, I just watch. "Oh, I'm sorry," she gasps, swiping her eyes dry. "They told me you would, but I didn't…"

"I'm okay," I say on reflex, wanting to comfort her. It isn't until I say it out loud that I truly realize this isn't heaven, or hell, or some other place the dead go. This is home.

Which is impossible.

Unaware of the way I've stopped breathing, Mom reaches over to clutch at my arm. The movement jars me, and agony radiates through my bones. "Oh, I'm sorry," she cries a second time, getting tearful again. "I forgot, how could I forget? They said you would be sore for a while. You had hypothermia." She notices that the news is on and fumbles for the remote on the side table. Blessed silence fills my ears.

"What's wrong with my fingers?" Despite my valiant efforts, a tear escapes. It quivers down and slips into my mouth.

"They said you might lose sensation in your fingers and toes. I'm so sorry." Mom's expression is twisted with anguish. It's probably not just for me—the newscast about Nick is undoubtedly on a loop. If the numbers were wrong for me, could they have been wrong for him?

"Where is he?" I ask. Fear coils under my skin.

My mom knows instantly who I mean; I see it in her watery eyes. "He's dead, Ivy."

"Then how…" I catch myself and stop. Swallow. "I need a mirror," I say evenly. Mom doesn't move. I say it louder. "Please, I need a mirror!"

Whatever argument she'd been about to make vanishes. Her purse must be on the floor, because she bends down. Moments later Mom straightens with her eye shadow case. Fumbling, she opens it and holds the tiny mirror in front of me. My heart rages against the wall of my chest as I stare. No. This is a dream, a delusion. But why isn't it ending? For an entire minute it's impossible for me to speak. I swallow again and again.

It's real. It's incredible. It's terrifying. It's wonderful.

The numbers are gone.

Mom is crying again. The case shakes in her grasp, and

I quickly look at the space above her head, too. Nothing. No numbers, just air. That's what was off about her. I feel dizzy at the rush of emotion. Joy, pain, elation, despair. What does this mean? Who am I, without that glowing timer? Where do I go from here?

The answers to those questions will have to wait, because Mom is still sobbing. "Look at me. Hey. *Look at me*," I order. She obeys, sniffling, and I shrug. "At least I still have them. Losing a little feeling doesn't matter, okay? All that matters is you're here." *That we're both here.* I know the words are a bandage on a gaping wound—Uncle Nick is still dead—but they're all I'm capable of right now.

Mom leans over to pluck some tissues out of a box by my head. "Lorna has been waiting just as long as I have," she tells me. "She's been making plans to pass the time. I guess she wants to open a club in Karlstad, complete with dancers and fruity drinks at the bar. She went home an hour ago to get us some clothes and more paper to write on." She utters a shaky laugh.

I process this with raised brows. It may not be exactly what I had in mind when I sabotaged my sister's website, but that's the thing—she finally has a goal, a dream that's all her own.

My mind is still spinning when Mom adds, "Also, they found N-Nick's will. He left me the diner." When I don't respond, she grapples for something else to babble about. "Myers is here, too. He's been sitting in the waiting room for two days. Along with most of the town, actually."

It's too much information. Out of those two sentences I only hear one word. "Myers is here?" I echo, sounding like a hopeful child.

She smiles and gets up. There are indents in the chair cushion where she sat all that time, waiting for me to open my eyes. "I'll go get him," she says.

"No, Mom, it's—"

"I need some time to freshen up, anyway." Mom blows me a kiss and disappears.

I lie there and just listen to the noises around me. Murmured conversations out in the hall, the wind pushing against the window, my own soft breathing. In, out, in, out. It's a reminder that it really happened and I survived when no one else ever has. It's not fair compared to people like Vanessa and Shannon and Miranda—their timers didn't start over. I know that no matter who I become or where I end up, I won't forget that.

The blizzard grows louder outside. It pushes at the glass and I watch the swirling gusts. This time, they can't touch me.

A sound makes my heart skip a beat, and I turn my head. Myers fills the doorway.

The sight of him nearly breaks me. I want to pour out all the pains I've kept locked inside. Some secrets, though, can never be spoken of, regardless of miracles or second chances. "I'm supposed to be dead," is all I say. My lips tremble.

Myers moves to stand beside the bed. His brown eyes pierce through me. He looks so tired, and his caramel skin is paler than normal. Once again, there are no numbers to be seen. "You were," he answers, brushing my bangs back. It calms a bit of the chaos inside of me. "When I pulled you out..." His jaw works, and he starts again. "I got a call from Amanda Ryan just as you were leaving the house. She told me not to let you out of my sight. So I followed you as closely as I could without making it obvious. I was there when you went into Havenger's, and when Nick went in a little later. By the time I decided to leave the car, you'd already gotten to the lake. I followed the tracks.

"When I found the place where the ice had broken, your hand was wrapped around the edge of the hole. I pulled you out and couldn't find a pulse. I thought you were gone. I did C.P.R. for an hour, or at least it seemed that long." Myers finally sits in the spot Mom vacated and says nothing more, does nothing more other than keep touching me. As if he's worried this isn't real, too. He brushes his palm over my arm, he trails it over my shoulder, he cups my cheek. He's so warm, always so warm. We are fire and ice.

Quiet descends over us, but words feel inadequate right now. I'm still trying to think of what to say when Myers brushes the wetness on my face away with the pad of his thumb. He tells me, grinning weakly, "You look better. Less blue. I was worried for a second."

With an answering smile, I raise my eyebrows. It's addicting, this happiness. I wish I could touch him back. "Just a second?"

His voice becomes a slow smolder. "A lot can happen in a second."

There are so many meanings to that, I can't catch and name just one. Rather than trying, I say, "Thank you. For saving me."

Amusement glints in his gaze for a moment, but it swiftly fades when he notices my bandages. "I should have gotten there sooner."

I instantly shake my head. "No. You got there right on

time." Belying this, though, I crack just a little—another tear falls. This one isn't borne from joy. I'm a teeter-totter, tipping back and forth between crushing anguish and manic elation. Suddenly there's a commotion out in the hallway, and I hear someone call my name. The voice is unfamiliar. Reporters, probably.

Myers goes to the door and shuts it. He returns to me and reaches for my hand, stopping himself at the very last moment.

Now I sob, the blow of everything feeling even harder when I see his fingers so close to mine but can't feel the warmth of his skin. It seems ungrateful and trivial, in the grand scheme of things. Yet I can't stop the wave of despair.

"Hey, hey." He leans over and presses a feathery kiss to my temple. He smells like cheap soap. "Everything will be okay. We'll figure this out. I'll be here. All right?"

With the tips of my numb fingers, I touch his chest. "You should go. Your sisters are probably worried and they need you."

Gently, so gently, Myers captures my wrist against his chest. His gaze is unwavering. "So do you," he whispers.

I stare up at him. The devastation still hovers as I think of Uncle Nick behind his desk, tapping his calculator.

"Do you need to rest?" Myers asks, beginning to extract himself.

"Not yet," I answer, pulling him close again, ignoring the pain. "We have plenty of time, you know." The words pop out. He smiles and doesn't argue.

The truth of it is hitting me now—*we have time*. There's no way of knowing how much, and that's the most beautiful part. I can finally have the life I used to let myself dream about in the weak moments. One that won't include walking out to the train tracks every Friday night, preparing goodbyes, watching Myers Patripski from behind a tree, or staring at Vanessa's old trailer. I can finally travel to that warm place or hop on the train.

Maybe my story really does have a happy ending.

But I can still hear the chaos waiting for me in that hallway; there will be questions and pain. Even though I loathed them, the numbers were the sun that my universe circled. Without them, everything seems uncertain.

This is how the rest of the world must feel.

"How are we going to survive it all?" I whisper, feeling like a ghost of the girl I used to be. I can hear Vanessa's voice whispering, *Live with me.*

My boyfriend kisses me. "One day at a time," he says simply. As always, he has the answers.

At that moment, sunlight bursts through the clouds. The storm is over. We turn our heads at the same time and admire the ribbons of yellow reflecting off the glittering frost. *One day at a time,* Myers had said. He was right.

It's already tomorrow.

Acknowledgments

This book would not exist without the amazing team that has dedicated their time and passion to it. Though I'd like to send everyone chocolate and diamonds as thanks, I'll start with acknowledging you here. My gratitude and awe goes out to:

Randall Klein, for championing this book and being such a patient editor. You've challenged me in the best of ways, and working with you has made me grow as a writer. Thank you for not batting an eye when our efforts demanded more time and more extensions. Without you, *Gardenia* would not be what it is now, and I'm proud of the result.

My agent, Beth Miller. I sent you this manuscript years ago, and though it needed a lot of work, you've never hesitated to dive in or put Ivy's story out there. It's difficult to believe the manuscript that's been floating through our inboxes since 2013 is finally in print! We did it! Thank you for being so dedicated and determined. It's been a wonderful six years and I can't wait to see what else we can do together.

The team at Diversion, for being so excited and so accommodating with deadlines. Sarah Masterson Hally, Eliza Kirby, Nita Basu, and Jaime Levine. You work diligently behind the scenes and don't get enough recognition from me. I deeply appreciate all you do.

Tanya Loiselle, for reading the first draft. You're never daunted by the mess, and you're always a text away when I need encouragement or second opinions. Thank you for your friendship all these years, Tiger.

Pintip Dunn and Natalie Richards, for such lovely blurbs. My heart leapt when I saw your names in message headings. I'm ecstatic and humbled that you read *Gardenia*, and I hope to meet you both someday to tell you in person. Thank you.

As always, to Emily Neuman and Jordan Kralewski. I'm not sure how I wrote books before I met either of you, but this trio has become a vital part of the process. Thank you, my best friend. Thank you, my partner. I love you two so much and can never adequately express how much your efforts mean to me.

And finally, to my readers. You waited patiently for this book, and I received an outpouring of inspiration during that time. Even the shortest tweet meant everything. I'm not sure how I got so lucky, but thank you.